Guy Who Knows

GUY WHO KNOWS

ISBN 978-1-66782-668-4

The sweetest smiles hold the darkest secrets.

— SARA SHEPARD —

Contents

Anonymous

Prologue

I am The Guy Who Knows—a real-life storyteller, resident of the Upper East Side, and admirer of the super ladies operating on the streets of the Madison Avenue.

This is not another gossip story; this is the best thing that ever happened to you!

You are probably wondering what this is going to be about. Unfortunately, I cannot describe it in a few words, but I can say what it's going to feel like.

Remember the first time you had sex? Bear with me here. Do you remember the sensation, the excitement, the butterflies, your feelings of what was going on, or who was doing what? Slowly, the unknown started to feel good. The heat began to rise, the sense of pleasure became overwhelming, and your tension built up until you finally exploded and released all your energy at once. Then you wanted to do it over and over again to keep feeling that complete bliss. This is what you will feel like when you're done reading these pages.

The ladies of the Upper East Side are rare creatures—like no other, even in New York City itself. You have your West Side moms and Downtown gals and Midtown fashionistas. But no one compares to the Upper East Side lady. These women live with a mission in their eyes and a target on their backs. Often, they make wrong decisions, leaving a trail of frenemies behind them. All is fair in love and war. And in this war, the stakes are too high. These women are either born into money or marry money. Whatever the case may be, they are not willing to let go of this money, even if the price is their own souls.

To be considered a true Upper East Sider, you must build the right size family, attend all the luncheons in your clique, shop at the right stores, eat at the right places, and get your hair done at the right salon. Then you must know how to throw and host a party—and any occasion will do! Even your dog's first birthday celebration is a good enough excuse to shell out a million dollars.

The most important thing for Upper East Side women is knowing how to play the game, how to pretend, and how to gain acceptance for themselves and their kids in all the right establishments and clubs. Do any of these things wrong, and you risk losing your social status and becoming persona non grata—meaning, you will have to relocate, shop, and dine below 59th Street, which is considered taboo for these Upper East Side ladies.

For those living in the kingdom of the Upper East Side, Madison Avenue is the only place to be. It is where the ladies get their shopping, dining, and beauty on. They need to be seen on the sidewalks of Madison Avenue or, more accurately, stepping out from their cars while their drivers hold the door as they enter the Chanel boutique on a causal Wednesday afternoon.

These ladies have it all—the husband, the family, the money, the social status, and the connections. When they want something, all they need to do is snap their fingers. Just like that! "Poof!" It is done. Yes, they live fairy tale lives, and they are all so happy.

But are they?

Behind every Botox smile and made-up face, there is a story dying to be told. These women hold more in their closets than pairs of Jimmy Choos and Birkin bags. They hold their secrets, desires, and the most intimate details of their lives. They have many skeletons that they tuck all the way in the back—in the dark where no one can see or hear them. But eventually, every skeleton wants to see the light of the day.

This is where I come in.

Who am I? You already know me. We have dinner together, sometimes drinks. I was there tearing up when your daughter got married, and I danced at your son's bar mitzvah. We shared that secret once, remember? I was behind you in the line at Sunset Beach brunch, and we definitely have pictures together from that crazy Playboy party.

I am everywhere and everyone. You might hear people whisper my name. You might even swear you know who I am. The rumors will start pretty swiftly, I imagine. But trust me, you will never know who I am until I want you to know—not even when your friends tell you they have proof of who I am. You see, I control this neighborhood. I designed it all a long time ago.

It is a new dawn on the Upper East Side. So wake up and smell the imported green leaves, because the tea is about to be spilled.

Close your shades, dim the lights, fill your glass with the best wine in your cellar. This shit is about to get real!

XOXO,
Guy Who Knows

The Lululemon Paradigm

Dear Readers,

It is a glorious day on Madison Avenue. The sun is shining high, the stores are well-stocked with the latest trends, and the ladies have just left their young ones with their nannies or sent them off to school.

Living on the Upper East Side means you must be fashion-forward. Your name must be on the contact list of every fashion designer—from clothes to shoes to handbags and diamonds, of course. The real necessity—almost a must-have item, a sort of admittance into Madison Avenue society is the Birkin bag. It is not just a bag. It is the pinnacle of social status, letting everyone know you are one of them. It says, "I can afford to be here, and I have no plans to leave anytime soon."

The ladies of Madison Avenue are expert shoppers. In fact, they even have a budget. That budget would fund a small country. A significant amount of their monthly allowance—aside from attending $10,000 a plate luncheons—is dedicated to fashion.

This is where things get tricky. At what point did Lululemon yoga pants become the new social status item on Madison Avenue? One cannot pass from 5th and 3rd Avenues without navigating a flock of ladies walking around in yoga pants. Apparently, if a lady is not wearing these pants at least every day of the week, she does not exist! Whether one actually does yoga or exercises is not important. One can wear them just because—and apparently the ladies must have a pair for each day. A lady must start her day by wearing them and instructing her driver to take her to the nearest Starbucks, where she will get her favorite venti-flavored coffee (skim milk, of course) or Juice Press, so she can cleanse her body with pre-made trendy green juice. You do not have to truly live a healthy lifestyle if you just pretend as if you are.

Parts of the flock will work out, sweating their asses off at Soul Cycle for about sixty minutes. Once the ladies are sweaty and gross, and before going home to shower, they rush over to their local beauty parlor to get their hair—which is now drenched in sweat and god knows what else—re-fluffed and re-blown. Re-blowing of the hair after a workout is always great fun for the stylist. Nothing better than to blow dry hair that is wet, filthy, and smelly. The visual effect of sweaty shirts and sweat drops still dripping down her face and neck is an added bonus. And the aroma is asphyxiating. One can literally fall to the floor over the fumes rising from dirty, sweaty hair being blown dry at maximum heat—a true pleasure. One should not miss the opportunity to experience it for themselves.

Wait, we got sidetracked over here! Let us roll back to the Lululemon pants and to my question, "When did these yoga pants become standard everyday outerwear?" With a closet full of designer jeans and pants as far as the eye can see, why must the yoga pants make an appearance every day? Even if it's for a casual breakfast at St. Ambrose or taking her baby with the nanny on a walk in Central Park, all while wearing yoga pants, as if she is about to work out vigorously. Yes, these pants are paired with brand name sport shoes, a $10k bag and a coat which could easily be the down payment on a new home. Still, social rules on Madison Avenue dictate that you will walk around all day in yoga pants! This is one mystery I have yet to unravel.

Now, these yoga pants come in all colors and patterns. Is it a window into a lady's mind that she wears a particular pattern to fit her mood for the day? For example, if she is wearing the design with scenes of Manhattan spread all around her butt and thighs, is it safe to assume she is about to explore the city using her butt as a map?

Another lady is wearing a storm and lightening pattern. Does that mean she is in a serious and not-so-great mood today—or simply giving us the forecast? Also, we have the beach scene with sun, blue skies, sandy white beach, and the ocean—all on one pair of yoga pants. Is it safe to assume she has a vacation on her mind? So many questions! I need answers!

Oh, my word. As I am writing these lines, I received an email with a 20% off coupon for Lululemon. Please excuse me. I simply must get online and shop before all the New York City patterns are sold out.

XOXO,
Guy Who Knows

Attack of the Clones
MADISON AVENUE EDITION

Dear Readers,

The Upper East Side is probably the only place in the world where money can't buy you class—or for that matter a sense of style. Yes, they will go to Bergdorf Goodman and drop $5000 on a dress, only to look like the neighborhood Madison Avenue hobo (who incidentally sits in a wheelchair all day long until the clock says six p.m., when he stands, folds up his wheelchair, and drives away in nice 2017 Nissan Altima). Who say L.A. is the Land of Dreams? Madison Avenue is where the magic really happens!

It just so happened when I stepped out my door one day I noticed two Upper East Siders who seemed to be on their way to SoulCycle, dressed in matching hats, coats, leggings, and boots and sporting sleek, smooth, dark hair. For a moment, I rubbed my eyes and thought, "Is it possible that I'm seeing double?" But I was not. Nevertheless, it was like seeing an amoeba duplicate herself. Looking closer, I realized that they'd shopped exactly the same! No doubt one of them bought something new that the other deemed worthy. When that happens, it spreads like ragweed during allergy season. They get on their phones immediately and order with overnight shipping so they won't be the odd one out. The most obvious one I've noticed in the last couple of months is a jacket you could get on Amazon for $100. Overnight, it seemed that everyone had to have that jacket. The Amazon jacket was the only one that mattered. (Forget the fact that they have Moncler jackets galore adding up to thousands of dollars in all colors hanging in their closets.) But this was the jacket of the moment.

BIRDS OF A FEATHER FLOCK TOGETHER. These words should be cast in iron and displayed publicly on Madison Avenue, right at the entrance to Bergdorf's. When it comes to UES hairstyles, our birds are no different. Highlights are the must-have color treatments and a wavy blow dry is the only style that exists. Anything else will get you enough sideways looks and fake compliments to ensure you'll be the object of gossip at the next Save Our Kids luncheon—which actually has no relation to the kids—but a chance to show we all have the same Birkin bag and yes, we're all rich enough to afford a $10,000-a-plate charity lunch where all that's on that plate are sparse salad greens and an oily dressing.

Then, of course, we have the denial stage: mothers wanting to look like their daughters, and daughters trying to look like their mothers. No, ladies, it is *not* cute to wear matching booty shorts, and let me tell you why. Your daughter is eighteen and hot. You, on the other hand, are pushing fifty and your cellulite is showing (I'm just saying). And when your eleven-year-old daughter wants hair highlights like you only because her friend got the same highlights as *her* mom, you should not encourage it. You should encourage creativity. And Heaven forbid if she cuts her hair shorter than the acceptable below-the-shoulder length. This move would be considered crazy and completely disconnected from the reality of Madison Avenue.

Clearly, yours truly has strong opinions, but I cannot help asking myself, "Is it finishing school that dictates all ladies ought to look the same?" No wonder we hear stories of husbands sleeping with their secretaries who (ladies, cover your ears) wear clothes from J.C. Penney and get their hair styled once a year at the most. Anything to break the monotony.

One cannot help wondering what makes these ladies with unlimited financial resources and armies of personal shoppers completely forego their individuality and creativity and become obsessed with all looking the same.

Oh well, you'll have to excuse me. I just heard Saks is having a sale, and there are several must-have items I simply must have so I can blend in with the flock. Toot-a-loo!

XOXO,
Guy Who Knows

Anonymous

Mrs. Dime

Dear Readers,

It is with great pleasure that I introduce to you Mrs. Dime. She is not an ordinary lady. She is the matriarch of her clan, a busy social bee, and an avid card player. Mrs. Dime is also older, so she has not only been around the block but also been part of old New York and the Upper East Side back when it was still classy.

Mrs. Dime plays cards as often as Catholics go to church. Playing cards is her way of confessing and getting more gossip from her fellow worshipers.

Her whole life revolves around her hair. Her hair maintenance schedule is set just like the four seasons, only she wouldn't last a full season without getting her "do" done. It is a steady stream of appointments: one week—a haircut, the following week—her color, then three—blow dries in between and repeat. Heaven forbid if one of her stylists decides to take a vacation during the standard routine. That would mess up her schedule entirely, causing the sky to fall over her Park Avenue building entrance. The woman can book six months in advance without blinking, YET, she confirms these appointments each time she calls or walks in the salon door. You're probably wondering why she has to call and confirm so often. For her, confirming her weekly schedule is part of her every-day agenda. If you are the lucky person answering the phone at any of her favorite spots, this how the conversation would go:

"Yes, Mrs. Dime, how may we help you today?"

"Well, I need to confirm my appointment for next week. And let me tell you why. My electrician said he might need to come check the connection on my wires because next month, I have a big din-ner for twenty people, so I have to get my carpets cleaned. Now, I can't have him come after they've been cleaned. Then, my chef has to start working on the menu, and I need to get my blinds cleaned as well. It is a disaster!" (You think I'm lying, right? I am not! Word-for- word, so help me God.)

Did I mention she is always on a tight schedule? Oh yeah, she must be taken on time. You see, she doesn't work, so in reality, she is rushing nowhere. However, she must be finished in precisely one hour! So the team, of course, works vigorously to make sure they meet her deadline just so when she's done, she will mention again she has to run, BUT not before she books another three months' worth of appointments—even though she has already booked and changed them about five times. Of course, if one of her friends walks in the salon door, she is no longer in a rush. I guess her next appointment to nothing just got canceled, so she may escort her friend during her beauty services and spend another full hour talking to her about grandchildren or her husband's business trip and why it's such a drag on her—which just reminded her that she has to book another appointment before her husband's business trip. So, we are back to square one because that will change the order of the other four hundred appointments she booked already.

After all is said and done, Mrs. Dime finally leaves the salon to continue doing nothing—but in a hurry, of course. She can't leave before she throws the staff a comment that if she stayed any longer, she would have to get her hair done again!

Do not get me wrong. I ADORE Mrs. Dime. She is a true diva who knows what she wants and when she wants it. No rain or storm will keep her from getting her hair done, especially if it's right before she must get in a car driving to the Hamptons or a plane flying to Boca Raton.

There is so much more to tell you about Mrs. Dime, but I feel this is enough for now—a good jump-start. The funny part is that she is not even in the top ten craziest ladies on the Upper East Side.

Stay tuned for more.

XOXO,
Guy Who Knows

Anonymous

The Story of Fluffy

Dear Readers,

Meet Sarah Daring, wife of Aaron Daring—a devoted mother of two beautiful girls and a hardcore New York City housewife.

Sarah has an army of people at her side: her stylist, whom she sees three times a week; her manicurist; her once-a-week tanning specialist; and her dermatologist. (BTW, if you ask her, she is not getting Botox. The occasional bump you see on her forehead is a spider bite.) Yes, Sarah is keeping herself well maintained as is fitting for a woman of her status, living in a penthouse overlooking Central Park South.

Sarah's daughter has flown the coop, and she's feeling a bit of an empty-nester. So what is a woman with too much time on her hands to do? For $6000, she buys a purebred puppy named Fluffy who has just graduated from doggie finishing school!

Fluffy is adorable, and while there are also many equally adorable dogs in shelters available for adoption into permanent homes for a nominal fee, it makes complete sense to Sarah to instead support an industry that abuses dogs for its financial gain. But I digress. . .

When it was time for Fluffy's first birthday party, Sarah decided that this event must be immortalized. She invited twenty of her closest friends who share the same dog breeder AND dog mother so all Fluffy's brothers and sisters could celebrate together—a family reunion, if you will. No expense was spared! A red carpet was brought in, and butlers offered pink champagne to the human guests and organic dog treats to our four-legged friends. Fluffy's party featured a photographer with a pop-up studio brought in to take portraits. Twenty dog walkers were hired to attend to the individual needs of each dog, while their owners continually relieved themselves during two hours of drinking, dining, and socializing.

The dogs had their choice of spending play time in the grand hall or sixty-minute appointments in the rooftop sunroom staffed with special doggy masseuses to take away their doggie stress and bring back their Zen. A unique selection of cold cuts and entrees were prepared by New York City's top caterers—not for the human guests but for the dogs. Lunch was paired with bowls of Evian water and served on fine china set on gold placements, all with a window view of Central Park South. Yes, it was every dog's dream come true, to live the Upper East Side life in a grandiose way.

Of course, our hostess did not let her guests leave without a parting gift bag containing homemade (not by her, but by the chef) dog cookies, a framed photo portrait of each guest posed with their dog, and a leather dog collar with their dog's name written in scripty Swarovski crystals.

It was indeed a party for the books! The doggies had a great time and went home to pass out from all the excitement. Their owners, still conscious, were now facing a perplexing dilemma: where to hang their new doggie portraits.

XOXO,
Guy Who Knows

Anonymous

Pills or Drinks

Dear Readers,

January in New York means winter in full force. It also means Madison Avenue going into SALE mode—emptying the shelves of the winter selection to prepare for the coming of spring.

During the winter months, we all must find our own way of dealing with the bitter cold that is an everyday reality. Some of us fly to Miami whenever we can. Some deal with it by binge watching favorite shows or choosing a local watering hole. Some of us even have secret sexcapades which will forever remain tucked away.

On Madison Avenue, where money is not an object and everything is a matter of want, the only real escape you can have is through pills or alcohol. Do not hate the dealer, hate the game.

Drinking is an acceptable activity in moderation at social gatherings. However, if you show up for school drop-off hammered by 8:00 a.m., it is frowned upon.

Pills. Well, let us not be naive. We all had our youthful years when we dabbled and experimented. For most, that's exactly what we did: experimented and left it at that. But for some of us, that dabbling became a vital lifestyle.

Allow me now to formally introduce you to Dorothy Love. Dorothy, by no fault of her own, is now seeing green Martians wherever she goes. She lives her life thinking she is invisible most of the time—a charming experience, I am sure.

Dorothy was born and raised on Madison Avenue. She leaped through all the necessary hoops to grab her coveted spot in a higher social circle. She got married, had kids, attended all the lavish parties and charity luncheons and shopped at all the right stores.

Unfortunately for Dorothy, her husband left her for the "old story:" Man hires receptionist, man falls in love with receptionist, man leaves wife and kids and marries receptionist. (That is the fairy tale Disney should tell!)

Poor Dorothy has checked the undesired box of being divorced with kids while her husband moved on to a better life somewhere over the Pacific Ocean. But not all was bad for Dorothy; she was lucky enough to be born into money and inherited millions that will allow her to maintain her lavish lifestyle. But that was not enough to keep her happy. Existing on the Upper East Side with no man or desire to date again and her overwhelming boredom forced Dorothy to search for another solution—one that could not be purchased from the shelves of Saks Fifth Avenue. Instead, her solution was to be found at her local Duane Reade with the help of the right prescription from a witch doctor willing to sell his soul for a shiny new car—even if that meant taking a perfectly healthy, bored, capable mom and turning her into a zombie.

Dorothy slowly became deranged, going from a vocal, outspoken, and active person to a slug leaving a trail of slime on the pavements of Madison Avenue. Her manner of conversation shifted into one where she believed people needed to be spoken to slowly and in a thematically inconsistent way. By that, I mean Dorothy would start a conversation about her dress and her next sentence would be about the fact that we put a man on the moon decades ago. She had lost her grasp on reality. Nonetheless, she is a sweet person. How many people do you know who can stare at you for ten minutes straight without saying a word, then ask you, "What day is it?"

Life at home was no picnic as well, especially for Dorothy's twenty-person staff attending to her twenty-bedroom home and catering to her every whim while her kids were at boarding school. The staff was having the time of their lives with this 24/7 live dramedy called Dorothy Love. She provided entertainment wherever she went. While she had no schedule and nothing to do, she always reminded people that her profession was psychiatry. One should not peek under that stone is all I have to say.

Dorothy kept to herself and stayed away from the social circle for two reasons. For one, she was not invited. For another, she simply did not remember they existed anymore. She was so disconnected with the world and herself that she used to claim she had stopped smoking, all the while holding a lit cigarette in her hand. The one thing Dorothy never forgot is to always look tanned like she just came back from a long weekend at the French Riviera. She was so on-point getting her tan that she went every three days. It reached the point where the most famous tanning facility on the Upper East Side—which caters to A-listers and socialites alike—did not know what to do when she insisted on getting all those sessions. Luckily for Dorothy, she was not a bad person. The tanning salon people loved her, so they gave her the feeling she wanted. They put her under placebo lighting which did nothing to her yet gave her the feeling she was still getting tanned.

All we want in life is to feel beautiful, and old habits do die hard.

In Dorothy's case, I believe she maintained her weekly beauty regime not because she wanted to look young and fresh, but because it was the leftovers of a life she once had. In those beauty spots she frequented, the people were always warm to her. Maybe it was because of her money. Maybe she even knew that and didn't care. Maybe it was because they remembered her in her glam days and genuinely liked and cared for her. Whatever the reason, being beautiful made her feel good, and that is something we all deserve.

XOXO,
Guy Who Knows

Girl Gone Wild

Dear Readers,

This is one of the most scandalous stories ever told in the United States. And little wonder it all started with an Upper East Side woman.

The Upper East Side is full of young, up-and-coming ladies—beautiful, bright, well-mannered girls eager to climb the social ladder. For that, they need to land the right husband who can present them with the said ladder before they can start climbing it—preferably in Chanel.

The hero of our story is nothing of the sort. Meet Lorelai, the latest edition of "girl gone wild" in New York City. Lorelai hardly deserves a second look. She is not well-educated or mannered. If New York City was a game of chutes and ladders, she'd enjoy being a player—even though luck is never on her side. Some people know when to call it quits, but not our girl! It feels like no matter how many times she keeps losing, she will continue to play the game. One must wonder if she will ever make it to the finish line, or simply keep sliding down the chutes and smacking her botched face against the pavement.

Unfortunately, her claim to fame began with some tragic circumstances. But our Lorelai is resilient and used her tragedy as a stepping stone. She was determined to make the Upper East Side her home. Her only problem was that she didn't really fit in with the usual crowd. In fact, she stood out more than a straight guy at a Celine Dion concert. On the Upper East Side, if you do not have the right social power or come from a prestigious family, you're a big no-no.

You see, Lorelai has no money and no class and does not come from the right family. What she does have, from her sketchy position at a New York private establishment, are good connections. Those connections allowed certain doors to open, giving her access to more influential people. How she gets the money to pay for her Balenciaga bag and her Lanvin shoes. . . well, let's just say that the movie *Pretty Woman* comes to mind.

Moving a little bit forward, one of America's biggest scandals breaks all over worldwide media. At the center of it all is our dear princess Lorelai, with improved facial structure and a new bra size, splashed all over *Page Six*. Overnight, Lorelai is the only name on everyone's lips. The media circled her as the new Britney Spears. Nothing else mattered now. After months of rumors and denials, Lorelai broke down and admitted the accusations. And while she did not break any rules per se, she was America's most-loved and most-hated woman at the same time.

Attention on the Upper East Side is never a good thing unless it is to announce marriage, acquisition, or the birth of a new heir.

Suddenly, the swamp of Madison Avenue was bubbling! Now all eyes were on Lorelai, and attention followed her everywhere she went. This did not sit well with the ladies, who quickly excommunicated her. Every important establishment and social circle was now closed to her. She was officially persona non grata.

The media eventually laid off our poor little excommunicated princess. But every now and then, they release a new item about her to keep the fire going, hoping the next big headline will come from her. Unfortunately, the media fails to do proper due diligence and only looks at the surface. A bit more digging on their part would unveil the truth, providing more than a few headlines. Luckily for you, yours truly has many little bees buzzing in his ear.

It appears that Lorelai—neither now nor ever—had a real dime to her name. Wherever Lorelai went, there was a gentleman to pick up the tab. While names were never given, credit card numbers and three-digit security codes were. A little more digging proved that Lorelai is more broke than M.C. Hammer ever was. Apparently, her apartment rent hasn't been paid in almost a year. The person who was supposed to be her best friend in the whole wide world got stabbed in the back—hard, and now is on the hook for paying her bills.

Meanwhile, Lorelai finds ways to fund her essentially extravagant lifestyle and shopping sprees. Currently, she's scouting around town like a tiger roaming the jungle, looking for a new man to get her claws into.

If the Upper East Side is a pound, beware. Someone is not locking the cages. The bitches are out on the loose.

XOXO,
Guy Who Knows

Megan's Potty Training

Dear Readers,

It is time now for an extra-juicy story. And when I say "extra-juicy," I mean that quite literally.

Please allow me to introduce Megan Long—famous outerwear designer by day, sparkling socialite by night. She lives in style on the Upper East Side, spending her days in Saks Fifth Avenue and her lunches in Freds at Barneys. Megan is a beautiful, six-feet tall woman with luscious hair and (sadly) a terrible nose job. But her sweet personality and innovative talent shine out. Unfortunately for her, she has one little habit that can't be overlooked, even for the brightest of personalities.

Picture this. It's a beautiful and sunny Tuesday morning in the Hamptons. For Megan, it's a typical day on the grand patio of her beach house. The patio has been transformed into a shooting set for her collection of outerwear out next spring. The team is working hard on the models. Megan has her own dedicated team of stylists who are applying themselves to making her look fabulous, working that luscious hair, and highlighting her cheekbones.

While Megan gets her makeup done on her favorite barstool, her makeup artist begins to notice a watery brown liquid leaking down Megan's thigh. He pays no attention until the leak becomes a full-blown waterfall, with clumps and all. And can you guess, dear readers, what might be running down Megan's long, shapely leg? I can, but will spare you the gruesome details and leave it entirely to your imagination.

Nevertheless, the artist keeps working diligently until Megan's makeup is complete. As she leaves the chair, she hastily disappears into the bathroom before participating in her big cover shot. Her makeup artist stands viewing the little liquid souvenir Megan has left behind like a tip on her barstool. Being a consummate professional, the artist removes the stool and thoroughly washes his hands. He then requests that the staff bring a new chair as he locks up the memory of this little incident in his mind for life (or at least until he met up with yours truly).

A couple of days go by. More photos are needed of Megan's spring collection. This time, the shooting location has switched to a professional studio rented for that purpose. Our dear Megan arrives on set and simply must use the little girl's room pronto. As she returns from the potty, a little bird suggests that her makeup artist go and check. Sure enough, in front of the same stall from which she recently emerged, he finds another of Megan's treasures, right on the floor!

It is well understood that Megan, like many Upper East Siders, has control issues. And like the true Upper East Sider she is, she faces those issues head on—by ignoring them completely.

My suggestion for Megan: maybe skip breakfast and instead get back to your Kegel exercises.

Please excuse me while I go take a shower. . .

XOXO,
Guy Who Knows

Anonymous

Blondie

Dear Readers,

The sun is shining, the days are getting longer, and the bees keep buzzing!

Oh yes, it's Springtime in New York—time for spring cleaning, bringing your spring fashions forward, and burying your Prada coat and Jimmy Choo boots in the back of the closet with the rest of your secrets.

Some secrets, however, cannot be buried forever. At one point or another, they will see the light of the day.

The next Superwoman I will introduce you to is a force to be reckoned with, and her name is Blondie. She is not your ordinary Upper East Side girl by any means! She is a full-time working woman, running her own company, and is highly successful in her field. If I didn't know better, I'd say she has her own pair of balls—but who knows.

That was Blondie before she had her lovely first-born son, birthing him at a more mature age than one might expect. At the time,

Blondie was married to her much-older hubby Stanton—until he left her for the nanny (minus the baby, of course). But that's another story, bees.

After a remarkably short divorce process, Blondie emerged with a substantial alimony settlement. Not that she needed it, because Blondie comes from money. However, she is a firm believer in the old saying, "Don't get mad—but do get everything!"

Post-divorce, Blondie eased into being single and all the perks of her new life. She moved to a lavish three-floor apartment on Fifth Avenue. Reserving the top floor for herself, she gave her new nanny strict instructions never to come up there. That way, her "men" and her nanny would never have an opportunity to meet, and history could not repeat itself.

If you remember my story about "drinks or pills," Blondie's choice was clear—imported vodka and lots of it. As her baby was fond of sucking on a bottle three times a day, so Blondie nursed herself on a bottle of Gray Goose. Oh yeah, Blondie indeed loved her liquor. So much, in fact, that walking a straight line proved quite the challenge.

One evening, Blondie returned to her Fifth Avenue residence from a social gathering, and it would appear to the casual observer that getting out of her limo and walking into her building was Mission Impossible. But Blondie, being the Superwoman she is, refused the help of her lovely doorman. Try as she might, however, she fell straight into the manicured bushes. When her second attempt to enter the building failed, her doorman saw that her humiliation was complete. He insisted on escorting her up to her very apartment door, where he delivered her into the loving hands of her nanny.

Dating was also new now for Blondie. Her taste in men is quite particular. The eligible must be over sixty, have white hair (an absolutely must), and must be boring (of course). She doesn't care about a great physique in her men, but they must have a vigorous libido, even if one needs his little blue pill to get things going.

For example, Blondie started dating Mike—a respectable, divorced hedge fund manager with no kids and who has a belly like Buddha (and the same amount of hair). One eventful night, these love birds went out and the drinks started flowing (among other things). One thing led to another, and the couple ended up on the private floor of Blondie's apartment, with Blondie bent over her balcony rail and enjoying the nighttime view of Central Park, while Mike enjoyed gazing at the secret tattoo on Blondie's right cheek—and his scrutiny was quite close, I might add.

But this shows you how fast fun can turn tragic on the Upper East Side. During a rousing game of "Mommy and Daddy," Mike passed gas—an act Blondie thought was completely inappropriate and disgusting. The game was over.

But in reality, it was only beginning. Mike declared war. Drunk and high, he decided to show Blondie how offended he was that she was offended by marking his territory—quite literally like a dog—ALL OVER her apartment. Their yelling was so dramatic that a not-so-close neighbor in the building overheard them and called the cops. The mayhem continued, with Blondie screaming her lungs out as Mike's full moon came out and he proceeded to leave his "stardust" all over her custom-made furnishings—her pristine white sofa, velvet ottoman, and a rare, hand-crafted silk carpet. (I'm sparing you the precise details, but yes, it is exactly as disgusting as you might imagine.)

The night finally came to an end as three cops escorted Mike out of Blondie's apartment in nothing but a silk bathrobe, and she became the talk of the entire building in a matter of minutes! The story hit the airwaves all along Fifth Avenue. Soon after, Blondie sold her place and moved to a more secluded townhouse, away from judgmental eyes.

What Blondie fails to understand is this—on the Upper East Side, my bees will follow her wherever there is honey to be made.

XOXO,
Guy Who Knows

Mary Had a Little Cow

Dear Readers,

It is springtime! The trees and flowers in Central Park are blossoming. Pollen is in the air, and allergy season is revving up, along with our ladies of the Upper East Side. The girls are ready to leave their winter tales behind them and get ready for the spring social season—which means parties, traveling, and even Memorial Day weekend in the Hamptons, a picturesque landscape of local farms with horses and cows.

Today's story involves a cow, and I suggest you consider this as a warning before heading over into crazy town.

Please meet Mary Middleton—not your typical Upper East Side lady in more ways than one. She's classier, more reserved, less flashy, much more sensitive, and completely off her rocker.

If her family allowed Forbes to feature them among the fabled "500," they would land on that list every single year. However, we will resist getting into why this is for the moment. Mary's style choices are basic: bag by Hermès, shoes by Chanel, diamonds by Harry Winston, the essentials really. But she wears it all in a subtle way, nothing too flashy or gawkish.

Mary is currently living in one of the fanciest hotels on the Upper East Side. No, she isn't vacationing there. She's only been building her dream house for the past ten years. Worry not, she isn't slumming. She lives in an exclusive three-story suite built just for her family and their four dogs.

Funny story: her husband thinks they have only one dog. Why, you ask? Because he agreed to purchase one dog and one dog only. Mary, being lonely in her enormous suite while her husband lives mostly on a different continent, has no problem hiding the additional pooches and pretends to her husband that they do not exist. Nearly three years ago, Mary's house was almost ready. It had all the standard amenities, of course—an indoor pool, a gym, a home movie theater, a tennis court, staff quarters, a guest living room, a formal living room, three kitchens, a formal dining room, a ballroom—everything a modest castle needs minus a moat surrounding it all.

But before they could occupy it, a small problem came up with the flooring. Mary discovered a microscopic crack that bothered her so much she declared they couldn't possibly live in such a house. Now I don't know if there was really a crack, a scratch, or if she's just a lunatic. But whatever was in the floor, it simply would not do! The contractor was instructed to start over and re-do all the flooring. According to Mary, simply replacing one offending tile was not a sufficient solution and would jeopardize the integrity of the entire construction.

When Mary is not checking her new house with a microscope, she has many other hobbies. She's interested in art, music, and looking after her kids—only now those kids are all grown up. Walk down memory lane with me, when her son loved basketball so much, she reserved a private basketball court for him at the bargain price tag of $3000 a day, five days a week. Currently, I suspect her day job is to monitor Madison Avenue and make sure everything stands as it should. Mary's daily routine takes her up and down the Avenue, all the way from 59th to 86th Street, day in and day out, all day long. It is commonly believed that this routine is the reason she remains in such great shape (always a plus when you live on the Upper East Side—not that anyone is judging, mind you).

Mary is a huge animal lover. So much, in fact, that on one of her trips to the rural Hamptons, she encountered a cow and fell hopelessly in love. A gentle soul like Mary could only make one choice: to adopt the cow! When I say "adopt," I mean this cow now has a better life than me. Mary's adopted bovine gets a monthly allowance of $10,000 for fresh, green pasture and its own special caregiver. The caregiver ensures Mary's cow gets regular exercise and plenty of fresh air and sunshine. Once a month, Mary travels to see her cow pal.

Now, I do not think it is crazy at ALL. In fact, I want to suggest to Mary that if she truly loves cows so much, I am happy to dress up as one, walk into her living room on all fours (when her husband is not home, of course) making mooing noises and chewing the grass. If the mood strikes her, she is welcome to try milking me for all I care. I will just remember to buy milk prior to our sessions and attach it inside my costume so she can have the full cow experience. I'm more than happy to oblige her in order to receive my monthly $10,000 check.

Overall, Mary is the sweetest person on the planet! Nice, kind, and soft-spoken. Yes, she speaks so softly you sometimes want to put a bullet through your head, and her OCD is off the charts. But hey, we've all got our quirks, right? Only she is looking at quirky in the rear-view mirror, and there are no signs of her changing anytime soon.

Think of Mary next time you're on Madison Avenue. If you see someone with an Hermès bag and Chanel shoes patrolling up and down, it might be her.

XOXO,
Guy Who Knows

Dear Diary

Well, hello there, Upper East Siders!

It's another beautiful day in New York City. The trees in Central Park are now in full bloom, and the streets are bustling with endless ranks of tourists who fill up the rooms at the Mark Hotel and shop Madison Avenue for overpriced handbags to carry back to their home countries as souvenirs of their trip to NYC.

On Madison Avenue, one of the most important things is to have your hair done. No matter what the event, you must have the perfect blow dry on top of the perfect cut and color!

If you've kept track so far, you know hair salons are the most important holy sites to Upper East Siders. One must attend them religiously or be banned and considered "free spirits" who care nothing about their looks.

Someone died and there's funeral to attend? A blow dry is the ultimate accessory to go with grief. Going into labor? Not before a quick trip to your hair salon! The last thing you want is your OB-GYN judging your poor hairstyling as you push the baby through your birth canal. Going to shop at Bergdorf's? Of course! Can you imagine the embarrassment if, as you shop, the store clerk notices your roots? Heaven forbid!

What happens if a lady cannot make it to a hair salon and do her daily worshiping? I hate to think of such a tragedy. Fortunately for the ladies of Madison Avenue, if you cannot come to them, they will come to you! There is no "No" on the Upper East Side. There is only the question, "How much?"

Meet Vivica Garcia Athos DeVille, an older lady—and I do mean old. Let's just say, strictly between us, that by the time Kennedy was shot (she also knew the family very well), she already owned half the real estate in Manhattan, compliments of old family money and three dead husbands.

Sweet Vivica has spent her life in the finest places with the finest people. With each husband, she became richer and richer until money was like stacks of Post-it notes on her kitchen counter. As time went by and Vivica got older (as happens with many Upper East Siders), she developed a habit of seeing her doctor for every problem and receiving a pill for it. This happened so much that, at some point, Vivica stopped leaving the house altogether, even for family or social events.

As time passed, she started losing her mind. So she began keeping a comprehensive journal to show her doctor on her weekly (yes, weekly) visits. Are you wondering what Vivica's journal contains? Let me tell you.

Her journal describes every day of her life in minute detail—what she ate, how it made her feel, what pills she took, how those pills made her feel, how she woke up, what she did around the house and anyone who was with her. Make no mistake, readers. Underneath the fog caused by her pills, Vivica still had a very sharp mind and could remember things that happened months and even years ago.

There was no real purpose for her keeping a journal, nor did her doctor request it. But that didn't stop her from endlessly writing in it.

The journal was not the only thing she kept in perfect shape. She kept her hair as well! By herself (without the aid of an assistant or housekeeper or anyone else), Vivica called her favorite salon to get her hair either cut, colored, or styled every week, even though she had nowhere to go and wasn't receiving anyone! Why? She lived in fear that she would unexpectedly kick the bucket and her hair would not be properly done.

Now if you're thinking Mrs. Garcia Athos DeVille just sat there while her stylist attended to her locks, you are dead wrong.

When the stylist first arrived in the building, he was instructed to wait because madam was not feeling well. After he was allowed to come up, they needed to find the right room with the right lighting for her styling session. The light was always different, because she never had her stylist over at the same time of day. And because she changed her furniture every now and then, that affected the lighting too (according to her). After all was said and done, it was time to start with the process—but not before Vivica gave explicit instructions on what she wanted, even though he's the same stylist she has employed for the past thirty years! Then she wants to instruct him on how to do it: how to hold the brush and where to aim the blow dryer. An average blow dry takes about forty-five minutes. Hers took about three hours (no joke)! Her stylist never got fed up with her because he charged an arm and leg, which she happily paid. Vivica was many things, but among that she was also one of the most generous ladies the Upper East Side has ever known.

To this day, she still lives in her UES apartment with her staff and gets blown dry while looking down on Manhattan from her forty-fifth floor balcony in a certain building on Park Avenue.

Personally, I like to let my own hair down. And the only journal I ever write in is this one, wherein I detail the fantasy lives and experiences of the great ladies of the Upper East Side.

XOXO,
Guy Who Knows

The Phone Whisperer

Dear Readers,

Springtime in New York is not only a great time for the trees and flowers to bloom. It's also time for the Central Park squirrels to emerge from hiding and invade The Great Lawn. Like these furry creatures, many elite Upper East Siders who fled to Florida for the winter are now scurrying back for the Spring social season.

I have the honor of presenting to you one of these ladies—Mrs. Blanche Rose.

Mrs. Rose is Old New York, involved with many charitable societies and a big philanthropist. She's a classy lady who wears only earth tones in heavy fabrics. Anything less than Chanel, Dior, or Hermès might as well be a uniform on a member of her household staff. Blanche is known for her heavy makeup and speaking in low, barely audible tones. If you're lucky enough to meet her for the first time and have a brief conversation, you'll assume afterward that you're going deaf, because the woman whispers everything. It is nerve-racking.

Blanche's whispering is also how she speaks on the phone. She often calls her many service providers—her florist, her baker, and her favorite restaurateur. Whoever answers her phone call gets the notion that Mrs. Rose isn't permitted to use her home phone, that she'll be severely punished if she's caught making outbound calls. She starts the conversation at a low volume and then goes even lower. It goes something like this:

"Hi this is Mrs. Rose I wanted to ask ‒ ‒ ‒

You cannot read it, right? EXACTLY MY POINT! One cannot hear her, either. One supposes that if her husband, Mr. Rose, ever caught her on the phone, all hell would break loose. This makes me wonder how that situation might unfold at the Rose home. Let's imagine it, just for a moment:

The scene opens.

MR. ROSE. (*catching his wife on the phone*) Are you on the phone? I told you before, you are NOT allowed to use the phone!

(*He strides across the room toward her, loudly pulling his leather belt off through the pant loops and brandishing it over his head. Mrs. Rose backs away in terror.*)

MR. ROSE. (*swinging the belt*) Come here! DON'T YOU RUN AWAY FROM ME!

Mrs. Rose. (*trying to shield herself from the blows*) No, please! I was only calling for my flower arrangement! PLEASE! (*Offstage, we hear an anguished cry of "Ahaaaaaa!" from the maid, pleading for Mr. Rose to stop the beating.*)

{END SCENE}

Being on the phone with Mrs. Rose is also no picnic for another reason. She takes numerous breaks between her words, as if these mental pauses give her space to wonder if she left something on the stove or forgot her laundry in the dryer (as if she even knows what laundry is). It goes something like this:

"Hi......this is......Mrs. Rose......" and so on and so on.

Her husband, on the other hand, is outspoken. He will tell you loud and clear what's on his mind whether you asked for it or not. I guess as a business tycoon and head of the family, he's earned the right. Mr. Rose is also the source of income for extended family members. In fact, wherever the family goes into town, they have the unrestricted use of several house accounts—Bergdorf Goodman for clothing; Frederic Fekkai for beauty products; and Ladurée, the French luxury bakery—to satisfy their sweet teeth.

A woman who joins the Rose family (by marrying one of their five boys) gains access to these very fortunate charge accounts. It is Mr. Rose's requirement that wives will not work and must stay home to attend to their husbands' needs. Rumor has it that each woman in the family is given a $50K per month budget for their own up-keep—clothing; shoes; perfumes and creams; makeup, manicures and pedicures; hair maintenance; and more.

Meanwhile, my own grocery store budget for the week is fifty dollars (coupons included).

The boys are nothing to write home about. The first born, Elbit, is the pride and joy of his mother. He's married with two kids and is an executive in his dad's company. Elbit attends every New York high society function with his lovely wife as his arm candy. Behind the scene, it's a different story—he's discreetly dating different women every night, then sporting his heroin-chic look the next day in business meetings, including dark circles under the eyes, complimentary of that special fairy dust.

Connor, the middle son, is also an executive in the family business. He married a woman who looks conspicuously like his mother (Did someone say "Oedipus Complex"?) and is constantly being told what he likes and what he needs to agree to by his wife, Kaka. In Upper East Side terms, it's true love at its best!

Not much is known about the remaining three siblings, except the fact that Mr. Rose keeps it that way, because these three have chosen a more carefree, downtown, liberal lifestyle (one of them is a well-known NYC party boy).

The princess of the family remains Mrs. Rose, quietly struggling for her right to use the phone and whispering her way through life.

XOXO,
Guy Who Knows

The Party Conundrum

Dear Readers,

Springtime on the Upper East Side is always joyous. With days growing longer and nights getting shorter, it's the perfect time to throw a party!

Who among us doesn't enjoy a good party? Great food, entertainment, social interaction, and copious free drinks that lead to mostly poor choices—like sleeping with your best friend's boyfriend (Search online for "Khloe Kardashian and Jordyn Woods"). Let's face it: we've all been there by making one bad choice or another.

On the Upper East Side, it's not much different, except the budget is unlimited and a birthday party to mark one's turning forty becomes a grand spectacle of wealth with three hundred of one's closest friends. The guests are mostly people they hate but must invite because it advances their social agenda. Yes, these parties are a sight to see: dancers with bejeweled titties, their bikini pants emblazoned with the guest of honor's name across their bottoms, a DJ flown in specially from Ibiza just for one night (at a cost of $250,000), sushi prepared by blind nuns smuggled into the United States illegally who pray as they prepare your dragonfly roll. The truth is, you only turn forty once (even if your fortieth was five years ago—but who's counting?).

What happens, though, when one guest gets really drunk, starts behaving inappropriately, and spills the beans about the host? Now this is where things get interesting. . .

Please meet Dina and Mallory. First, allow me to tell you their stories. Both are up-and-coming new-money girls from the slums of New Jersey. Both got lucky and landed rich husbands. They moved to Park Avenue around the same time, where they proceeded to get reservations at all the hot spots in town and worked their way onto guest lists for the most luxurious social events.

Their next step was to build their legacy—aka their Infantry of Screaming Babies. This legacy-building admitted them to an exclusive club of mommies who do nothing all day long. They have armies of nannies to take care of their young ones while their drivers drive them from place to place. Real family time comes in the form of nightly dinners together. That is, of course, if Dad is home, which in most cases he is not, or if Mom is available for her kids, which is also not likely as she's usually on a group call with her galfriends, tossing down her third glass of chardonnay.

Dina threw a party for the ages to celebrate her sixth anniversary with her hubby, Mr. Who Is Sleeping With His Assistant But It's Okay Because He Just Bought Me Diamond Earrings From Van Cleef & Arpels. Invitations were carved in wood and hand-delivered to each guest. A staff of 150 was hired to attend to every need of their 400 guest friends. Palm trees were flown in to The Plaza Hotel, creating the perfect "evening on beach" ambiance—even though the temperature out on the street was still below fifty degrees. Guests were instructed to dress in beachwear. Giant screens projected video over three hours of ocean waves and sunsets. The menu was fusion cuisine—Cuban meets Kentucky Fried Chicken.

Tour the bar lounge with me, where the magic is really happening. Specialty cocktails were created in honor of Dina and Mr.'s favorite flavors. We have to navigate through a mile-long display of empty glasses before we reach the bartender, where we must scream our order at him over a sea of drunk ladies yelling, "Oh my God, you look so thin!" "Oh, stop it! I'm as fat as a broomstick! I just passed by on my way to the bathroom to throw up dinner!"

Halfway through the party, Mallory gets tipsy. Now when I say "tipsy," I mean she literally finished a bottle of vodka all by herself (#girlpower). Drunk, courageous, and very honest, she started to tell whoever would listen that Dina was the biggest... oh, let us say biggest "honeysuckle" in college, and the only reason she married her husband is because she found out about his indiscretion with another man. Mallory goes on to say that Dina did not care about Mr.'s indiscretion. Instead, she saw the opportunity to "get him" and told him if he didn't marry her, she would tell his family all about his same-sex adventure and he would be banished. No one knows for sure if all this was true or not. However, as is often said, where there's smoke, there must be fire.

Dina naturally did not care for Mallory's revelation and asked her to calm the f**k down and leave. Dina's ultimatum did not help the situation, though, and Mallory got even bitchier. She started to insult Dina, her family, and every choice her dear friend from the slums of New Jersey had made in her entire lifetime. Mr., who saw the whole thing unravel, decided to spring into action. He whispered a warning in Mallory's ear—if she didn't grab her driver and leave immediately, she would wake up tomorrow as a Page Six headline. Whatever else was in that whisper was enough to scare Mallory out the door—but not before she spilled the beans on another small and fairly harmless secret. Now Dina's pre-college substance use was information widely available to the public.

Mallory's driver did not return her to her Madison Avenue penthouse that night. At the instruction of her husband, she was driven instead to the airport. From there, she was flown to a brand-name rehab facility to deal with her own apparent substance use.

Mallory returned to Madison Avenue six months later—only to pack up her family and leave the Upper East Side for good. To this day, no one knows what secret Mallory is hiding, but something tells me we'll find out sooner or later.

And if you're wondering about Dina's husband, yes, he's still sleeping with his assistant. Did I mention his assistant is a man? Oops, that little detail must have slipped my mind.

XOXO,
Guy Who Knows

The Stripper & The Beast

Dear Readers,

Lovely Fall in New York.

The nights are chilly, the air is crisp, and high heels are slowly being exchanged for ankle boots. Our dear Upper East Siders are back from their summer homes and readjusting to life in the city. The social calendar is filling up quickly, and "save the dates" for next year's weddings and parties are already in the mail.

Like every Fall, new faces are appearing among the old faces on the Madison Avenue and are being added to every doorman's journal. New families are moving in. New couples are buying into Park Avenue. And Europeans, of course, who love to spend time in Manhattan's elitist area, are looking too. Fall is definitely a real estate broker's favorite season—between the quiet summer months and the standstill winter market where all the deals get signed and commission checks get distributed. UES real estate brokers are like cats guarding the homes from unwanted mice and making sure other big, fat cats get the right pads. But sometimes, the cats drag in something really unwanted—like dead bird. Or, in our next case, a stripper and her beast.

Meet Leanna, Midwestern born and raised. Had never even seen New York City. Doesn't even know that "Ave." is short for "Avenue." Leanna has two kids from two different guys (No judgment, please! Just sharing the details). She has the IQ of a potato BUT is sweet as honey and perky as a kid in FAO Schwarz. Her expertise is dancing on tables, dancing on poles, lap dancing, being naked as much as possible, and performing science experiments on herself with recreational and not-so-recreational drugs. Yes, Leanna is a proud stripper—and not the kind you see in a Manhattan gentlemen's club, but more like those in the sad movies about small towns with girls just trying to make a living dancing in some hole in the desert. Before she met her husband, she spent her nights dancing on strangers' laps and finishing them off in their cars out back. But then her husband came along, and now she finishes other while he watches.

Keep reading.

Her current husband, Jedediah, likes to embrace a more natural lifestyle. No hair cutting, no shaving, no deodorant for that matter. His own fashion choices resemble those of a street bum looking to score drugs on East 86th Street. Through god only knows what illegal business, he had managed to acquire small fortune. Nothing impressive or major in Upper East Side terms, but somehow, he became the proud owner of two residential buildings in the worst of shape on 3rd Ave. ("Avenue," in case Leanna is reading this). Jedediah acquired these buildings when he moved to New York with Leanna, after sweeping her off her feet—or, more accurately, taking her off stage from the stable where she was working as a stripper. He packed Leanna and her two sons and drove—yes, drove—all the way to New York City.

Birds of the same feather flock together. And it's true what they say: every pot has a lid. This happy couple believes the Earth is flat and that our government is hiding alien starships in our backyard and insists on being part of the movement to uncover the truth—or maybe freeing the aliens. I am not entirely sure.

If that's not enough, get this. Leanna might have lucked out by moving to the Upper East Side. By complete coincidence, she was seen in few of the right places. She has no idea she was in way over her head. She tried throwing parties, but it was always the wrong kind of party. The only ones who attended were service people she came in contact with or strangers she met on the street who were fooled by her charm. No one who attended one of her parties ever came back again.

She invited guests to witness their hostess pay a call girl to sit on her sofa while Leanna is—how shall we say it?—tasting her clam chowder. Of course, Leanna's husband is there watching the whole time, not only paying for but also encouraging the behavior. On top of that, living on the Upper East Side caused Leanna to realize she needed to get her breasts enlarged (again). Not sure if it's the fashion or the fact that most Upper East Side ladies have the flat chest syndrome, which works to their benefit. They can wear oversize, unbuttoned blouses without worrying about "nip slip" incidents. But not our Leanna. She needed bigger, more extravagant breasts.

We are not done.

Her son, their pride and joy—well as they say, the apple doesn't fall far from the tree. Now to be honest, I am not sure if her son is gay or not. And not that it matters, but when he has older guys paying for his things, my eyebrows get raised. Is it that he doesn't get enough of an allowance? Or is it that his mother doesn't know what her son likes to play with? This is one skeleton that has not yet revealed himself completely.

Back to the husband and the fact that he is a slum lord. He keeps his buildings in such horrible condition. Jedediah rents to people he can take advantage of. He's practically running a drug playground in those buildings. It's not too long before Leanna's drug use and sex shenanigans become too much even for her. She checks herself in to a three-month rehab program—but not before she went around town notifying everyone that she was heading for rehab.

When it comes to fashion, Leanna definitely has her own style: a tight, see-through, girl-next-door look—even though she's pushing fifty. With her style, there is very little left to the imagination. And while some men might find her sexually appetizing, the ladies stay as far away as possible. They don't even exchange the fake pleasantries which they are so good at.

I am pretty sure by now you understand Leanna is not representative of the Upper East Side. However, she does reside in a condo within its boundaries. I'm sure I can't imagine any co-op approving this family, no matter how much money they have.

Leanna is really nice person. She's just in the wrong zip code trying to befriend the wrong crowd. And trust me when I tell you that her days are numbered. If there's anything the Upper East Side loves, it's a good scandal. One is sure to come with Leanna that will force her and her beloved and unique family to pack their bags and get on the next commercial main-cabin flight to Middle America, where not only will they feel they belong but also they will actually be celebrated.

I tried pole dancing once. Apparently, I have weak knees.

XOXO,
Guy Who Knows

Anonymous

The Good Wife

Hi, Busy Bees,

HERE'S another batch of fresh honey to serve with your afternoon tea. And get your reading glasses on—'cause this batch is coming to you straight from the Queen B herself.

Edith is an Upper East Side fashionista. Like many, she's a skinny bitch (a perfect size zero) with long hair (highlighted, of course, and blown out to perfection). She's married to a successful businessman who isn't so easy on the eyes but still charming at heart. They have two children.

Our story begins when Edith discovers that her husband Edward is having an affair with his secretary. A poor, delicate flower, Edith couldn't handle the news, and, overnight, turned from a cherry blossom into a pussy willow. She demanded that Edward move out immediately, while she rushed to the nearest psychiatrist for a full course of a prescription antidepressant that would tranquilize a horse. True, the meds calmed our poor girl down, but went too far, turning Edith into a virtual clump of mud, barely able to speak or express emotion.

On the Upper East Side, the worst thing that can happen to you is to disappear from society. Edith was still there, but also not there. Under the influence of her magic pills, she continued living as a shadow version of her former self, a skinny ghost drifting around Madison Avenue getting her blowouts, using her soon-to-be ex-husband's credit cards for revenge shopping, and telling her sad story to anyone who would listen. She didn't want or need a response, but simply continued touring her free one-woman monologue show on the sidewalks of the Upper East Side.

Time went by. Edith's shrink figured out how to regulate her meds. She bought new clothes and found a new look, and, armed with a new haircut, our girl began to piece her shattered life back together.

At first, it's pretty gloomy. Her kids are all grown and off to college. Edith sits all alone in her eight-bedroom apartment on Park Avenue with nothing to do and no one to talk to but her housekeeper. Then she finds exercise—something she thought she should have been doing all along. She hired a personal trainer to work her ass off in her home gym. That is exactly what her trainer did, three times a week, IN HER BEDROOM. Do you think she was ashamed of her behavior? Absolutely not. She was merely proving to her husband that two can play at this infidelity game.

The way I see it, why not? In fact, Edith got a free pass for life. She's rich, skinny, not young but young enough, and has no small children weighing her down. I say, "Go out, have a fun, shop, live, date, fuck till you can't walk anymore! Who the hell cares?!" But clearly, she doesn't share my devil-may-care attitude. On the contrary, the more she sees pity on the faces that surround her, the more she recognizes her life right now is a big disaster that needs fixing! Meanwhile, as Edith continues doing squats on her trainer's pelvis, Edward is going out of his way to try to win back his estranged wife—even buying a brand-new apartment and putting the deed in her name and paying for a trove of extravagant jewelry Edith picked up at a private sale at The Mark Hotel.

Edward's efforts did not go unnoticed. After two years and countless dollars spent wooing her back, Edith finally agreed to move in with him again. Two caveats: they sleep in separate bedrooms, and Edith is still heavily medicated. Life goes on.

And Edith's trainer? He still works the Upper East Side, making his rounds and stretching ladies in the comfort of their bedrooms. Oh, sorry. I meant their "private gyms." My bad.

Excuse me while I go to work out—

XOXO,
Guy Who Knows

Anonymous

The King & Queen

Dear Readers,

Today we are going to discuss the power couple who presume to be the king and queen of the Upper East Side.

King is a powerful businessman with a hand in everything who thinks he's God gift to womankind. He perceives that anyone outside his immediate (and royal) family was born to bow, kneel, and serve him and his queen.

Queen is an airhead bombshell with nothing on her mind except being rich and playing the trophy wife card wherever she goes. Like King, she also thinks she is second only to God. (Interesting, because she came from nothing and married up.) But now that past life is behind her, and anyone who doesn't have millions in their bank account isn't worthy of her friendship—not even her own sister.

In fact, when her sister was in deep financial trouble, and Queen could easily have helped her out with only the change in her pocket, she chose a different path. Queen demanded discounts on her sister's behalf wherever she could, just to avoid having to pick up the tab. Blood is thicker than water, but apparently not nearly as thick as a hundred-dollar bill.

Queen's sense of entitlement knows no boundaries. She enjoys making the joke, "No husband in the world would survive more than one credit card cycle of my spending"—as if one must be on a mission to spend NASA's annual budget in a one-afternoon shopping spree in Saks Fifth Avenue.

Let's talk about her children for a moment. The boys are charming, educated, well-mannered, and undemanding. However, they live under the rule of Queen's iron fist and need permission even before purchasing a simple Ralph Lauren t-shirt. Anyone who dares offer the boys any kind of advice is deemed by the Queen an enemy of the state and must be immediately destroyed.

Their girls are being groomed to rule the kingdom one day and all the minions within it. If anything is not to their liking, or their subjects are not acting as they should, they should expect to feel the heat of Queen's wrath upon them instantly. It's widely known among those who serve the Queen on Madison Avenue that "no" is never an appropriate answer. If Her Majesty should ask for the moon, one must reply "How soon do you need it, ma'am?" If the moon is then presented and is not to the Queen's liking, it must be removed quickly and trashed—preferable along with the offending servant who brought it to her in the first place.

Oh, and if you happen to tutor for one of the Royal Children, don't ever ask even for a glass of water. To be a tutor is to know one's place in the Kingdom, in their case standing and waiting endlessly in a designated area without chair or bench to lean upon until the Prince or Princess is ready.

Queen's loyal army of friends have more fear than love for Her Majesty. To their way of thinking, it's better to be at the right hand of this She-Devil than in her destructive path. One word from the Queen and it's "off with your head!" You are cast out of the social scene, just like that. Even if King decides to flirt and be touchy-feely and completely inappropriate with another man's wife, it's okay! He's King, minions! One must absolutely not address the incident head-on, for overnight, one's husband's business would suffer and rumors regarding his wife would spread like fire in a dry corn field, leaving no choice but to flee the Upper East Side and live below 59th Street—an area which Queen considers to be No Man's Land.

What Queen doesn't know is that her loyal army of friends is also her worst enemy. Behind her back, these bees buzz about her secrets in hushed tones. They dish about every move she makes, the King's indiscretions, and they laugh over her style sense and the shallowness of her conversation. In conversation, her topics are always monotonously the same: what to wear to the next event, where to shop, and what bright futures her children have in store for themselves. Yes, yes, it is always about her! There's no room for anyone else to talk about their own lives because the Queen has no interest in them. All she wants to know is who buys what from where, and who is dating whom in case she needs to forbid it.

When her best friend's husband's shady business dealings—which she knew about for years (and even the King had a hand in them)—became public on the front page of The New York Times, Queen immediately disassociated herself from her best friend and, in fact, was heard stating out loud that she barely even knew the family.

The King, of course, encourages all this behavior. In fact, he has a list of demands for his Queen. After all, the Queen is a public figure who must represent the King at all times. Therefore, she must always be well groomed, with perfect hair, makeup, and nails. Furthermore, she must always dress in heels and carry nothing less than a $30,000 handbag. She must shop daily at high-end boutiques, with three assistants dedicated to her and her only. The Queen must always be chauffeured around by her personal driver. Taxis or Uber are strictly taboo. After all, they are transport for the masses, not for our Queen. Even though her manicured hands have never done actual volunteer work, her name is listed on the board of every major charity as a top donor, just to let people know she is the Real Bitch, bitches.

Yes, our King and Queen indeed rule the kingdom. Rumor has it that they intend to expand their royal territory very soon.

Still, one cannot help recalling the ancient phrase, "The bigger they are, the harder they fall."

XOXO,
Guy Who Knows

Andre & Andrea

Loyal Readers,

It is a beautiful spring day in New York City, and our busy bees are at it again. One in particular is "at it" more than others.

Please meet Andrea Anderson. She is a beautiful mid-forties mother of one. Andrea is skinny (thanks to anti-anxiety pills) and tall (thanks to eight-inch heels) and has gorgeous blonde hair that she bought and paid for herself (sort of). Ms. Anderson—and yes, it is a Ms. and not Mrs.—because sweet Andrea never got married. "But you wrote that she has a daughter," you must be thinking, and you would be right to question that. On the Upper East Side, a single unwed mom is not a sight you see every day. Allow me to elaborate.

In her younger years, Andrea had extremely specific taste in men. For some reason, she found married men more attractive than single ones. We are not judging! (Well, fine, maybe just a little bit.) And it just so happened that she got acquainted with Mr. Andre DeVille. Andre, an extremely wealthy and successful investor, had made millions when he was still in his twenties. While his financial background was very solid to begin with, it was now exceedingly solid. Of course, Andrea knew that and could not resist flirting with him. She saw him as a fitting choice for matrimony, as fitting as a white glove fits the hand of the Queen of England. The only problem was that there was a Mrs. DeVille in the picture.

Andrea and Andre started seeing each other in secret locations and hotels across Manhattan. Our dear Andre started flying away "on business" more frequently than ever. Now this wasn't his first affair. However, his encounters with the ladies were usually quite short—and sweet and lucrative for them. There was never any emotional attachment. Andre is a serial womanizer, and the fact he had a wife and three kids never seemed to stop him from being who he is.

But this affair was different. Andre and Andrea actually developed feelings for each other. While Andre remained focused on business and family life and was completely fine with the current arrangement, Andrea wanted more. Very gently, she began trying to push Andre into divorcing his wife so he could be with her full time. Push came to shove, and she threatened to go public with their love story. For the first time in her life, she was sick of hiding and lying to people she cared about. She wanted Andre to make her an honest woman. In my opinion, her wanting to be made an honest woman was quite a reach, as if one were reaching to the moon, something possible only with an exceptionally large telescope.

From his side, Andre did not appreciate Andrea's demands. He made it abundantly clear that he would not leave his wife and kids for any women EVER. He might be a cheater, but believed that a divorce would destroy him, his family, and his reputation. He was ready to cut Andrea loose if she ever made this kind of request again. Finally, Andrea fully understood there was no way they would ever be a real couple, no way she would ever wear the coveted title of "Mrs. DeVille." She felt Andre slowly slipping from her long and well-manicured (which he paid for) fingers. At this point, Andrea backed down—but only to re-assess the situation. A crazy mind that works nonstop will eventually find a crazy—though not unheard-of—solution. It was then that Andrea pulled out one of the oldest tricks in the book.

Andrea got pregnant with Andre's baby. She did not tell him until three months had passed so he could not force her to terminate the pregnancy. Clever, shrewd girl. When she did break the news to him, he was not happy. Not even one bit! Now he understood this woman would go to any length to keep him by her side. Regardless, at the end of the day, Andre is a businessman. There is no deal he could not close, and so he flipped the tables on Andrea.

First, he announced that even with this baby in the picture, he still would not leave his wife and kids. He further informed Andrea that he would take no part in the child's life. It could grow up without its father and that would suit him just fine.

Andre didn't completely give her the cold shoulder. He made her an offer she couldn't refuse, dumping millions on her in exchange for absolute silence on the matter, demanding that she never revel his identity as the child's father and that they—Andrea and

Andre—would never meet again. If she refused his offer, Andre threatened to spread rumors about her that would slam the doors of society in her face and turn her into a persona non grata. And she would never see a dime from him. Even if forced to spend ten times more on lawyers, he would make sure that she would be the embarrassed one, not him. Andrea had no choice, and she accepted the deal. Before she even had time to process what had happened, she was summoned to an office building in Queens the very next day to sign the settlement papers. That very afternoon, Andrea became a multi-millionaire.

Though Andrea was sworn to secrecy, poor Andre forgot that it is the Upper East Side and there are bees everywhere who like nothing more than to find a nice flower they can suck the good stuff out of, turn it into honey, and buzz around the hive, all the way over to the queen bee, aka ME.

Today, Andrea's beautiful daughter is almost a woman. However, she is being kept away from the streets of the Upper East Side. This is mostly because Andrea does not want her daughter to meet her real dad by accident. As it so happens, she looks exactly him. But at this point of her life, this is one stone she is not ready to overturn.

Only a handful of people knows this little Greek tragedy, but now you know it too!

You'd think Andrea would have learned her lesson, found a single man, got married, and stayed away from married men. But NO, she didn't. Today, she is not married and is still dating married men. To be honest, though, as a multi-millionaire, these days she dates anyone she damn well wants.

I am off to change my Facebook status to "MARRIED" and see where it gets me.

XOXO,
Guy Who Knows

Anonymous

Mirror, Mirror on the Wall

Dear All,

Today I would like to introduce no one. Instead, I share with you a bit of Madison Avenue lifestyle, with an emphasis on style.

Before we move forward, you must understand that Madison Avenue life can be very demanding, and there is a price to be paid! The necessity to always look fresh and young beyond your age is constant. It's not a matter of "Do whatever makes you feel good." It is a matter of following social protocol, or others might think you cannot afford to be part of influential society. And let me tell you, no Upper East Sider wants that.

There are many cases of ladies bitching and complaining that all they want to do is wrap their hair up, wear sweatpants, order Chinese food, and disappear into the night, into their homes with their families (where of course there is a full staff standing by to cater to their every whim). The irony is that the Upper East Side is where it's supposed to be all about having the luxury to choose what to do, where to eat, and what to buy. Yet, the reality is that one does not have the luxury of having one's own mindset in doing what makes one feels good (aka the wrapped hair and sweatpants).

That choice comes with an even higher price tag, even for this crowd. Alas, money and status are truly a double-edged sword.

You see, on the Upper East Side, it seems there is always someone watching. One cannot walk into Starbucks to get her favorite vanilla latte without being dressed head-to-toe in Chanel or Christian Louboutin. One must appear as if one were attending a royal welcome for the Queen. Things get trickier if your Instagram account claims you're a style icon of the Upper East Side, but your choice of patterns is often misguided and dates back to the 1990s. Unfortunately, bringing those looks back today doesn't make you stylish. It only makes you look desperate. Or, in the lingo of social media, you're #nostyle.

On the Upper East Side, there are many magazines, craftily designed by boutique owners and fashion editors, to sell more products. The store owners publish one socialite magazine for free (or practically free), while the editor in chief gets free services or items in return for this free publicity. Yes, it's called bartering, and it's a perfectly good business arrangement. However, when the flock gets sold style, based solely on what someone in charge gets for free, it is no longer legitimate style. It is merely what one girl gets for free and is now stylishly shoving down many other girls' throats. The sad fact is that most of the ladies drink it up as if it were water from the fountain of youth. In reality, it is nothing more than Hudson River water in a fancy, environmentally friendly glass bottle.

We have not yet begun to scratch the surface of what it means to live on Madison Avenue. If you think it all ends with fashion and style choices, you are dead wrong. There is hair color to consider, the right doctors, the right fillers, and, of course, the estheticians.

Isn't it ironic? On the Upper East Side, where money is no object, one's options are still extremely limited.

Off to read all about the new styles and trends for 2020!

XOXO,
Guy Who Knows

Anonymous

Numbers Game

Dear Everyone,

The holidays are upon us! The streets of the Upper East Side are becoming a playland for those who dare to cross the boundaries of Second and Third Avenue and stroll for fun on coveted Park Avenue. There they observe an array of oh-so-bored doormen longing to be with their families. But they remain on the job, despite the holidays. Heaven forbid, what would happen if one of the lady residents should need her doorman to open the door and he wasn't there? (and yes, I clearly state "HE," because I have yet to encounter a single doorwoman on the Upper East Side). Oh, the horror of having to open your own door or hail your own taxi!

But let's not talk of such trauma. It's the holidays after all, and I have an incredibly special lady to introduce: Dori Dorfman, wife of Sam Dorfman.

For Mr. Dorfman, Dori is Wife Number Three. She is young and educated and comes from a good family. She's involved in her community and pays homage to all the essential charities. Along with her dear husband, she is raising one son—which is unusual on the Upper East Side. As you know, more children equal more wealth, right? So why did Dori have only one child with Sam?

The answer is simpler than you might think, and it's actually a smart move on Sam's part. In fact, you might say it's his way of securing his own future.

When it comes to wives, Sam definitely has a type: YOUNG. He meets his wives when they're at the peak of their youth and marries them. For a few years, he has fun parading them around as his newest, youngest trophy wife. Later, when they hit a certain age, Sam tells them, "Thanks so much for playing, darling, but I'm getting off this ride."

The son Sam had with Dori makes number seven for him, meaning that the alimony-plus-child-support he's already paying is substantial. And because Sam already knew where this was heading when he married Dori, he decided one son would be quite enough, thank you very much.

With a strong prenup agreement and great lawyers on Sam's side, the Dorfmans are now officially divorced. Dori is basically penniless. However, on the Upper East Side, "penniless" is a relative term, and Sam's newest ex is still doing better than 90 percent of the rest of the US population.

Still, Dori hasn't given up hope. She has so much to offer! With sagging breasts, a receding hairline and an abrasive voice rivaling Fran Drescher's, she is shopping around to become the trophy wife of someone in a pool of rich men who are sixty-five and older (true story). But so far, no luck.

And Sam, you're asking? He is happily remarried to a stunning Brazilian woman in her late twenties, and the two have a son together. As I write this, they are still married, so congratulations are in order—especially for Sam. The Brazilian is his youngest wife yet.

This is my Christmas gift to you. Happy Holidays!

XOXO,
Guy Who Knows

Anonymous

Whose Husband Is It Anyway?

Dear Readers,

Winter in New York is a magical time. One of the Upper East Siders' favorite Sunday winter activities is grabbing their family, grabbing hot coffee, and heading to Central Park for walking, sledding in the snow (if there is snow), or simply walking the family dogs and taking photos.

Winter is also the time when romantic movies fill the theaters. The story I have for you today is taken straight from the Hollywood studios—but better because it takes place on Madison Avenue, where life is one big never-ending movie. In this winter cold, put your warm hands together for our star, Kelly Lullaby.

Kelly is a traditional lady, part of an old society of ladies who pledge to stay young at all costs—even if the cost is drinking juice made from crushed snails. If your hair looks luscious, your skin is tight, and you're skinny as a broomstick, then life is good and nothing else matters! These women are called "Glamazonians."

Even on the Upper East Side, there are levels of glam. To be at the top level, one must have the perfectly decorated home in a coveted zip code, a driver, a chef, a household staff, a personal assistant, social status, the right connections, perfect kids attending perfect schools, and of course, the PERFECT husband who pays for it all.

The question at hand is this: What happens if one of the Glamazonians loses her most prized possession—her husband? Now she is forced to live on a budget. Worse than that, she must attend social functions alone. Oh, the horror! This is a really sticky situation to be in. Even worse, if you are a crazy lady and have that reputation. However, if you are a Glamazonian, there is always hope. There is always a fool out there with more funds than brains who can ignore your shallow personality and see you as who you pretend to be—young, fun, and flawless.

Enter Kelly. Through no fault of her own, she went back to being "Ms.," rather than being someone's "Mrs." Kelly had a childhood friend named Simone. The pair grew up together, vacationed together in the Hamptons, and even shared family vacations to other destinations. Simone had her perfect husband, kids, address, and more. She was a true friend to Kelly when the latter's marriage crumbled into pieces, like a chocolate mint on Christmas Eve.

Simone was swimming in money. However, she was no Glamazonian. She was a family gal, attending to her house and family religiously. She even invited Kelly over to her lavish home more frequently after her marriage fell apart to preserve a sense of family for Kelly's children. Sadly for Kelly, it only reminded her of what she had lost. Your need to know this before we continue. On Madison Avenue, there are no sacred cows. All is fair in love and war—especially when it is the love of money and power, and the war is to get more of both. On with the story. As I mentioned, the visits Kelly and her family made to Simone's house rubbed Kelly the wrong way. She grew increasingly tired of being alone and being someone's charity case. So she did what Kelly does best. She aimed her youthful appearance and fake personality at the one man on Madison Avenue who should have been considered taboo: Simone's husband, Ford.

The target was clear. Kelly was armed and ready. Her hair was slick, her nails were done, and her makeup flawless. She began casually visiting Simone's home when she knew Simone was not there. Then, she began attended the same social gatherings where Ford would also be in attendance. Her goal was to look appealing and attractive to a married man, take an interest in his work, and pay attention to his other interests. She got him to laugh, making sure she smiled a lot when she was around him. The rest is biology. Ford was easy prey, and it was only a matter of time until he fell into Kelly's web.

The high point of the scandal was a three-day weekend in the summer. While Simone was attending to her garden at the family home in the Hamptons, Ford and Kelly were doing some gardening of their own back in the city. The exact details of their glamorous three-day weekend in the Plaza Hotel's Royal Suite will remain the Upper East Side's best-kept secret. All you need to know is that they decided to keep their romance under the covers and west of 5th Avenue.

In the city, Kelly graciously agreed to help Ford deal with being separated from his wife and their kids. She provided him company and warmth so he would not feel so alone. The time was right, and Kelly decided to move forward with their relationship. Kelly took Ford to hers and Simone's favorite beauty parlor in one of New York's most prestigious and historic buildings. There, she gave the waxing lady specific instructions on what to wax to satisfy someone else's husband! This was a declaration of war on Simone, and it did not go unnoticed by the watchful eyes of the Madison Avenue clan. Soon after, the bees were buzzing and chatter about the new taboo romance had spread all the way to Southampton.

At this point, there was no denying that the affair was out in the open for all to judge. Upper East Side clans were forced to choose sides. Ford, of course, moved in with Kelly, who asserted her dominance on Madison Avenue by establishing rules regarding where Simone was allowed to be and when. The mandate was that Simone was not allowed to be within 200 feet of Kelly's location. Moreover, Kelly declared what had previously been their beauty parlor as her territory, forcing Simone to find a new one. The climax of it all came one day when Simone was in a pinch and needed to get a haircut for herself and Ford's son. They came to the forbidden beauty parlor and managed to be serviced, and then disappear moments before Kelly walked in. When Kelly heard about this, she was so furious that the Botox almost melted off her face! To prevent this situation in the future, Kelly went so far as to forbid the salon owner from having Simone at the establishment. If it happened again, she swore she would leave that salon and take her entire Glamazonian clan with her!

Simone was never seen in that beauty parlor again. In fact, she became persona non grata on the Upper East Side and remained so until she moved all the way across the bridge and through the tunnels into a world unknown (aka anywhere outside of Manhattan).

All is fair in love and war.

XOXO,
Guy Who Knows

Anonymous

Living in the Thunderdome

Loyal Readers,

Today, I want to discuss phobias, and how certain people can take their fear a step too far. Please make sure you're sitting down before reading these next lines.

Meet Betty. Betty comes from a prominent family and was born into money. She has no concept of what things cost, how money works, or even how much she has. All she knows is that when she wants something, she gets it—no matter the cost or how ridiculous the request.

You're probably wondering what the difference is between her and any other Upper East Sider with a trust fund or Black American Express card, and you would be right. Where the playground is Madison Avenue and the cash flows like grains in a sandbox, there isn't much difference. But what is unique about Betty is the fact that she is a germophobe of the highest order.

Betty loves her beauty regimes. But she refuses to walk into any beauty salon and use any of their tools or products. However, this will not prevent her from looking like the best possible version of herself!

For example, her nails. She likes to get a manicure and pedicure once a week. When the manicurist—let's call her Paula—arrives at Betty's home, she is instructed to wait in a special sterilized room before she is allowed to enter the main house. In said room, Paula must change from her own clothes into the uniform provided. She must place her shoes in a sealed bag and is required to spray herself with disinfectant spray. Paula is forbidden from bringing any tools or bags with her into the main house. When Paula is ready, she is escorted to a special waiting room with a bench, where she must wait until Betty is ready.

When Betty is (finally) ready, Paula is handed a brand-new, inside-the-box set of tools for performing her services, including new bottles of polish! Upon completion of Betty's nails, her dedicated housekeeper removes all the tools, inserts them into a sealed bag, and immediately removes the bag from the premises. Nothing can be reused!

I am not done. When Betty has a meeting, she of course has a hair stylist come over to style her hair. Yes, Kelly, her dedicated hairstylist, must endure the same process as Paula. To save time and answer your question, anyone from the outside world must go through the same disinfection process before entering the house! (That includes her husband and her two kids.)

Back to our story. Betty gets her hair done and leaves for her meeting. When she returns home, she herself must be sanitized as well, so she immediately gets in the shower. But Betty being Betty, her hair must always be done to perfection. Thus, she has Kelly, her stylist, return for another blow dry a mere two hours after she got the first one done!

When it comes to her hair, Betty is not messing around. She needs to have it styled at all times of the day—even if that means having her stylist arrive at 6 a.m. to wait for Betty to wake up! More often than not, Betty has Kelly over for a fresh blow-out and then completely ignores her. In that case, Kelly still must not leave the house until Betty's hair is freshly blown and styled. That, my friend, can leave Kelly waiting, sometimes for three or four hours. Neither Kelly nor Paula nor any other service provider can leave until Betty says so! Sometimes, another situation arises for Betty, after Kelly or Paula have already waited several hours. Betty decides to change her plans, or cancel them, or simply decides she's not in the mood to see people. She then sends them away!!!

However, Betty is not a monster. She was raised as a princess who gets whatever she wants and whenever she wants, and everyone must do what she wants as long as she is paying them. And paying she does! Betty is extremely generous with her service people, and even admits to them in private that she's happy to pay them whatever it takes to accommodate her unusual situations.

Which is why, on Madison Avenue, everyone wants to cater to her. However, only a few do. Betty picks her people with tweezers and a magnifying glass. If you cater to her, consider yourself lucky—as you would if you had the privilege of catering to Queen Elizabeth

II.

Sadly, since COVID started, no one has heard from Betty. It is rumored that she is living on a private island, completely secluded with only her closest people and staff. Not even those who are closest to her ample staff can confirm her whereabouts or well-being.

This guy is wishing her lots of Zen, as I am sure she needs it. To all the rest of you, please stay safe and healthy.

XOXO,
Guy Who Knows

Miami Bound

Dear Readers,

We can agree that the past year has been tough on all of us. Some have been hit harder than others. Upper East Side residents have indeed been hit, but let's just say hit differently.

"How so?" you ask. Please allow me to elaborate.

While most of the country was struggling to keep their jobs and support their families, Upper East Side families were struggling to stay together indoors. (Imagine cabin fever, only the cabins go for twenty-seven million dollars.) So instead of living harmoniously (or not) in their duplexes and triplexes and townhouses, they decided to flee to their mansions in one of two popular COVID-escape destinations—The Hamptons (obviously) or Miami.

This fleeing naturally causes havoc in their lives, as it necessitates leaving behind their adored trainers, stylist, hairdressers, and other staff members who could not afford to get up and go along at a moment's notice.

One example is Emily Biller.

An Upper East Sider born-and-raised who chose to live below the conventional border of 59th Street, our Em decided to pack up her husband, kids, and nannies; cram them into her private jet; and head down to Miami, where she could live a more carefree life. Problem: What is poor Emily to do without her army of people who make her look decent?

Luckily, our Emily is extraordinarily rich—somewhere between Batman and Scrooge McDuck—and she has no intention of letting this silly world pandemic mess up her daily routine. And just like that, an apartment was rented overnight. Em's hairdresser and celebrity personal trainer were flown down to Miami—also on the private jet—so that her life-affirming morning ritual of lifting five-pound dumbbells and getting her blowout (only to have it frizz after five minutes in the Florida humidity) can continue uninterrupted.

Emily did have to cough up quite a bit of cash for all this, so it's only natural she would get said trainer and stylist to sign a confidentiality and noncompete agreement while in sunny Miami. Sensible guidelines, like no dining in public restaurants with a lot of people (who knows what could slip out in conversation?), and no training or styling of anyone else. Period. The end.

Fortunately, readers, yours truly has eyes everywhere from Maine to Monterey. Wherever the clan goes, there I will be to see and tell you all about it.

Exclusively for the clan in Miami: While we do understand the pandemic is a huge inconvenience for your Instagram status (did someone say paid followers?), your audience does appreciate all you do to keep us informed on your life and—pandemic be damned—to be reminded how well you focus on the important things—like which couture dress is fitting for which sycophantic charity event. That kind of sparkling social media content is a welcome distraction from our layoffs, COBRA (Consolidated Omnibus Budget Reconciliation Act) payments, and the eviction notice that was just unceremoniously slipped under our front door.

There are more tales to be told of Emily in Miami (which sounds strangely like a sitcom from the early nineties), but as a wise man once said, "Don't bite off more than you can chew." Patience, my dears, all in good time.

I am off to check flight deals.

XOXO,
Guy Who Knows

The Salon Experience

Wakee-Wakee, Upper East Siders!

It's time to STRAP ON our Jimmy Choos and sport our Birkin bags. We're about to do some religious worshiping today!

The Upper East Side is a wonderful collection of cultures, ethnicities, and religions, each with their own uniqueness and pride. While we have a difference of opinion on whose way of life is better, there is one holy place that everyone—from men to women, young to old—attends religiously: their beauty salon.

Oh yes. The beauty salon is the only place where everyone has a common interest. All want to look their best. They visit the hair salon more frequently than either Shabbat night or Sunday service. They beg, plead, and pray for their stylist to make them look like time has passed over them. They're willing to pour tens of thousands of dollars into these salons to make those prayers come true.

On Madison Avenue, there are many beauty salons. However, there is one that is usually the talk of town, one that furnishes the essential drama by being the place to "see and be seen." This salon is a micro-universe of the Upper East Side and is unlike any other. Talented as the staff may be, "professional" is a mere title, and everyone who works there will attest that there is no better professional on the premises than them! And they do mean just them—singular, not a plural. Each stylist believes himself or herself to be the best and knows the best and all their other colleagues are simply lagging.

This lovely micro-cosmic salon is the place frequented by a few of the characters you've already met in these pages. But the more interesting characters there are the stylists themselves.

It's only right to give respect to the man who started it all—pure of heart, deceptively good looking though not the sharpest pencil in the bunch. You often see him at social events, trying in vain to rub shoulders with the rich and famous when it is clear he will never really belong to the Upper East Side clan. The UES ladies do enjoy spending time with him. And yes, he does do house calls—if you know what I mean (and I'm sure you do).

One of the most diva-ish characters is the salon manager, who struts around like a peacock. Instead of talking (and again, like the peacock), he screams. Instead of asking, he gives commands. He's often rude and sarcastic and can be too honest for his own good. He has put his foot in his big mouth more than a few times. For ladies who are generally accustomed to being treated as queens and having everyone suck up to them because they have money, his brutal honesty is refreshing. If you show up late on him, he will not be shy about screaming at you in front of everyone—even if your husband owns half of Manhattan.

Here's the thing: the manager is not mean-spirited. It's just that his mouth filter is broken, and therefore, he says everything that comes into his mind. It's not on purpose. In fact, some have been known to deliberately taunt him just to elicit his signature sharp-tongued and snarky remarks. On a more positive note, he is also well-known for making the impossible happen. When a particular princess walks in without an appointment and wants everything done to her simultaneously (and completed within one hour), he is her man.

Trust me, he is far from the most dramatic person there. Meet one stylist of foreign descent who once upon a time moved to New York to become a glamorous stylist and rub shoulders with the A Listers and the beautiful people. He's now blowing the hair of the old and lonely, those who are not fond of change and have sported the same hairstyle since giving birth some forty odd years ago. I guess the apple doesn't fall far from the tree, as he also dresses like his grandfather (in literally the same orthopedic shoes), and his mood swings are like New York weather. You can read the forecast, but you never know what you'll actually get.

Now let us talk about the Upper East Side's best-kept secret, the waxing lady. Lady Wax knows what she'll charge you for her services even before she starts by evaluating your handbag, your shoes, and your jewelry. (Everyone knows she knows everything about everyone on the Upper East Side.) Once the waxing room door has closed, the lady's G string comes off, and a good waxing session begins, the gossip starts flowing faster than beer on Saint Patty's Day. There is not an affair on the Upper East Side Lady Wax is unaware of. And no one, but NO ONE files for divorce without talking to her first!

Then there's the "Mamma" of the salon. She is a stylist who has outlived her heyday, but she can still twirl and curl. Already in her sixties, she looks forty. "But how?" you ask. Well, she could never afford Madison Avenue plastic surgery prices. So once a year, she flies down to Mexico, returning a month later with a tighter face, uplifted boobs, and a freshly plumped ass—perfect for her salsa-dancing nights on the outskirts of Queens.

I almost forgot to tell you about the makeup artist! Often when a stylist engages in their craft upon a client's head, they remain silent or engage in polite, sparse conversation. This superstar artist sees each client as an opportunity to share every possible detail of her life within the allotted time. Yes, her makeup skill is celebrated internationally, but the real art is her ability to condense her life story into one makeup session. Luckily, I draw my own brow and apply my own blush, because there is not enough Advil in the world for the headache you receive free of charge from any makeup session with her.

While the list of interesting characters who patronize this magnificent and beautiful salon goes on and on, yours truly can only spend so much time getting his hair done, because I'm also trying to catch all the skeletons lurking on Park Avenue. It is safe to say that this place has provided more scandals on the Upper East

Side than any other salon and is no stranger to *Page Six* writers (or readers).

Equally colorful as the staff are the salon's clients. While most of Madison Avenue can be seen dressed in Chanel and Lanvin from head to toe, the clients who frequent this parlor dress in Lululemon. From their pricey, sweaty bottoms all the way to their messy tops, their obsession with their hair is borderline sociopathic. One client yells, "Is she ready for me?!" as she bursts in the door, signaling that she must be taken RIGHT NOW, even though she will then spend one hour glued to her cell phone talking with a friend. Another client calls the manager over just to swear to him that she's not like all those other Upper East Side girls, that she is better, saner, and not demanding. (Never mind that she makes these protestations to said manager while getting her hair, nails, and makeup all done at the same time).

For me, the cream of the crop is that client well in her seventies. She walks in wearing tight leggings. Before she even says, "Hi," she readjusts her stretch pants over her full-figured body, a move which always reminds me an over-ripe banana trying not to burst from its peel.

This salon is one divine house that is open daily and always happy to accept new worshipers. And me? Personally, I think a more suitable name for it would be the Looney Bin, because everyone there is certifiably fucking insane. But then again, what is life without a little drama?

XOXO,
Guy Who Knows

The Story of Lala Falula

Dear Readers,

It is a glorious winter in New York. COVID-19 may have chased our dear ladies away from the pavement of Madison Avenue. The pandemic has left baristas all over the Upper East Side wishing for their swift return—so they can hear all about these ladies' lives while they're simultaneously screaming into their AirPods and waiting in line for their favorite matcha latte.

Run as far as you wish, ladies. But do not forget, the skeletons in your closet will follow you wherever you go, and I will follow them. The next skeleton is the somewhat tragic story of a mom whose appearance is everything to her—even at the cost of her son's mental health.

Meet Lala Falula. She is your average Upper East Side mom: Soul Cycle and Juice Press in the morning, getting her hair done at Rita Hazan, then shopping at Bergdorf's, and lunch at Avra. Lala is known for being overly attached to her phone. In fact, it is exceedingly rare if she is not on the phone when you encounter her. Her preferred method of communication is apparently sign language—the Falula version. One never knows if Lala is conversing with you or talking on the phone because she likes to stare you dead in the eye while yelling into her headset. Her specialty is walking into any establishment in New York while screaming on the phone, expecting the business staff to read her mind and serve her (as if one has crystal ball for the madness that goes on in her head).

While Lala does not have a job per se, it does not mean she is not busy. Her normal schedule consists of talking for two hours on each corner of Madison Avenue north to 82nd Street, dressed head-to-toe in Prada and Chanel, from 9:00 a.m. until 5:00 p.m.

Lala has three kids. One of her boys—her pride and joy, let's say—has some issues. What do I mean? Well, we all have voices in our heads. But for some, these voices are louder than for others. Now her boy has the charm of a can of worms, but it's not his fault. Still, his dear mom decided to do what many on the Upper East Side do. She swept his deep psychological issues under the rug—metaphorically speaking, of course. She wouldn't know a broom if one hit her in the head.

There was a major incident one time at his school that came after long line of small mischiefs. The school decided to expel him and asked his parents to find a different academic facility that better fit their son's needs. Dear Lala refused to hear anything of the sort. She begged the school to keep her son. After numerous pleas and arguments, the school caved in and agreed. However, their caving did not occur until our Lala agreed to a sizable donation to build a whole new wing onto the school, just so her son can stay at what she termed a "normal kids' school."

Oh, and one more thing. Skeletons are not the only things hiding in the closet. It seems that for now, though, that her first-born pride and joy will keep them warm. One can only imagine how Lala will handle the inevitable grand coming out. But let me tell you that this will be one topic she will leave out of her extensive phone conversations.

All skeletons are bound to see the light of the day—usually sooner rather than later.

XOXO,
Guy Who Knows

Anonymous

"What Do You Mean He's Not Available?!'"

Dear Readers,

Another beautiful morning on Madison Avenue. I am fortunate to introduce two great ladies today: Pipa Norton and Mindi Arch.

As you know, life on Madison Avenue is no picnic. There are brunches to attend, sample sales at The Mark Hotel one should not miss (even if it means postponing a visit to a relative who is clinging to his life at Lenox Hill Hospital). Social norms dictate that you must be seen at the hottest new designer's stores, stocking up on all of someone else's favorite things because now, they are your must-have items. And of course those beauty regimes that cannot be postponed under any circumstances! Looking perfect takes commitment, as you are about to find out.

Pipa is your modern-day superwoman. Her water broke, and she rushed to the hospital—but not before stopping at her favorite waxing place to get her bikini area done because, according to the whisperers, Pipa declared, "There is no way I am having this baby without a clean exit area."

The poor waxing lady was petrified as she waxed a nice landing strip to show Pipa's baby the way out. The waxer claimed she saw the baby's head and was afraid she might pull him out with one of her waxing strips! On Madison Avenue, one gets what one wants when one wants it, no questions asked. And if you were wondering, Pipa had a beautiful, healthy baby delivered by a doctor, not the waxing lady.

Meet Mindy Arch—Madison Avenue born and raised. She tried to get her blow dry 'cause she had an important and boring dinner for three to attend. And of course (as dictated again by social norms) she had to get her locks straightened. Nothing wrong with that. We all want to look our best for our friends of over forty years, and why not? But Mindy wanted to book a stylist who was scheduled to be out of the country at the time. One might think the artistic people who beautify these classy ladies are entitled to some time off. One would be wrong; Madison Avenue has its own rules. Mindy was shocked to find out her stylist was gone! Her Manolo Blahnik heels started shaking beneath her. Who will do my hair for this uneventful dinner? she thought after trying to communicate to the poor soul who answered the phone. "What do you mean 'he's not there?' I really need my hair done! Can he fly back earlier for me? Can you ask him? I really need to get my hair done!" As if there are not a million places on Madison Avenue to get one's hair done. Apparently, taking straight natural hair and making it straight again is no easy task, and her stylist's vacation really messed her up. "It's really annoying and messing up my whole plan!" Mindy laments.

Eventually, she rescheduled her dinner and her hair appointment for two days later—when her stylist was back to holding a blow dryer in his hand instead of a traveling bag.

Can you relate to Mindy? Or Pipa? Perhaps both? I know if I had a social gathering with friends, I would have checked my stylist's availability before I RSVP'd. Not to mention that if by some miracle I could give birth, I would choose to get my kooch ready beforehand! It's not like that baby is going anywhere!

Life is but a series of choices.

XOXO,
Guy Who Knows

Anonymous

The Maid's Tale

Dear All!

Valentine's Day may have come and gone, but do I have a love story for you.

Meet the Koopels. Jimmy Koopel is a successful stockbroker with the reputation that he can smell a hot stock like a cat can smell canned tuna a mile away. His gracious wife, Jamie, is an art curator for one New York City's more notable museums. Together, they are a power couple—some say the original power couple, before the term gained wide usage thanks to Brad and Angelina. In fact, it would appear that our dear Mr. and Mrs. Koopel and Brangelina have some similarities.

Jamie met Jimmy while he was still married to his former wife, Jenna. Jimmy cheated and lied to his wife for months before his best friend James—who always had a thing for Jimmy's wife—broke the gentleman's code and told Jenna all about her husband's affair. Unlike Jennifer A., Jenna took the news pretty well, and let me tell you why.

When Jimmy and Jenna met, they were a couple of kids from good families with a comfortable income. However, they were neither rich nor New Yorkers. When they got married, Jenna's dad pushed to have prenup for the young couple. One stipulation of the agreement was that if they were ever to divorce due to Jimmy's infidelity, Jenna got half of everything.

Years passed, and Jimmy became wildly successful. There were days when he made a million dollars just sitting in his office eating lunch. When Jenna found out about his cheating, she was not upset. To her, she just won the lottery! Before, she was an indentured socialite who had to attend all the New York charitable events and write checks from her husband's checkbook to keep them in the social swim. Now she doesn't have to do that anymore. She has all the money in the world. Jenna can now shop, eat, and travel the way she wants without a man or New York society dictating her every move.

Thanks to the prenup, it was very quick divorce. All Jenna had to do was prove Jimmy's cheating, which wasn't hard. A small bribe to one hotel concierge and a little security camera footage of Jimmy kissing another woman in the hallway and, "Voila!" Divorce! Back to the new Mrs. Koopel. Same but different. Jimmy's new wife Jamie and his former wife Jenna are both blonde, skinny (but not too much), tall, and gorgeous. You cannot help gawking when they enter a room. But unlike Jenna, Jamie loves working and being active and making a name to herself more than she loves being someone's missus. She has thoughts and opinions that she's not afraid to express. And while she is attending all these society luncheons and events, she isn't just a member of the audience paying

$10,000 for a plate of salmon fillet decorated with an asparagus spear. She helps organize these events and brings in big donors who support the cause. She is truly a force to be reckoned with.

On paper, Jimmy and Jamie were the perfect couple—madly in love, rich and powerful. What singles them out in their neighborhood is the fact that they have no kids. They have complete freedom to do as they please. It is good to remember that we're still on the Upper East Side, however. And as such, looks can be (and often are) deceiving.

In reality, Jimmy is a workaholic who doesn't leave the office until hours after the market has closed. Jamie keeps a busy schedule of meeting after meeting, trying to acquire more donations and more art for her museum. The couple does attend every party together, flashing their pearly whites for the cameras of the society magazines and bidding on charity items they do not need. Everything for them is lah-dee-dah on the outside. Their problems are only evident when you peek inside their five-bedroom, three-story penthouse overlooking Central Park that includes a swimming pool, an indoor tennis court, and yes!—a grand ballroom that can be used for any occasion.

Sounds lovely, yes? Well, there's one big catch. Jimmy's rule is that he does not want any household staff arriving prior to eight o'clock in the morning or remaining past six o'clock in the evening. Jimmy values his privacy. He does not want his staff around 24/7, determined not to live the Upper East Side life to its fullest potential. Jamie, a Manhattanite born-and-raised, does not agree with that concept. She wants around-the-clock care. Unlike Jimmy's first wife, Jamie was born into wealth. For her, the household staff are like friends—caring for all your needs. Servants are those to whom you can tell all your problems. This problem sharing had always been a struggle for Jamie when she spent time at home with Jimmy, for they rarely communicated. He had his work and she had hers. The passion that ignited their love affair had burned out long ago, and their relationship at present was little more than a business arrangement. Even their sex life was practically an arrangement, occasionally satisfying each other's basic physical needs but little more.

Jamie felt so lonely. Of course, she couldn't say anything to her friends, knowing that if she did, Madison Avenue would be buzzing with the news the very next day, leading to rumors and more gossip she feared would hurt her reputation and ruin her career. Therapy was out of the question, because she believed psychoanalysis was a waste of time. Still, she had to find a solution to her loneliness. Having an affair was not an option either, because she really didn't want a lover. She only needed a friend.

So what did our Jamie do to get herself a friend? She made a secret arrangement with one of her maids, Jinny. After six in the evening (Jimmy's household staff curfew), Jinny would hide in one of the storage rooms—a room Jimmy was sure never to look in. After Jimmy retired for the evening, Maid Jinny would emerge from hiding and spend girl time with her friend Jamie. But how, you ask, did Jamie make sure Jimmy would stay in bed so she could have her secret meet-ups with her maid undisturbed?

Simple: she drugged him. When I say "drugged," I admit I'm being a bit dramatic. But in a way, yes, she did, because she crushed up several sleeping pills in Jimmy's pinot noir every now and again when she needed Jinny's company.

One night, Jamie and Jinny were up extremely late. It was a week before her museum's huge charity event, and the pressure was on. Jamie desperately needed someone to talk to, so naturally she had put Jimmy to sleep in the usual way. But all went haywire when the sound of a broken glass woke Jimmy up around one in the morning. Walking butt-naked around the corner to investigate the noise, who do you suppose Jimmy encountered? Yep, his beloved maid, Jinny. Jimmy is doubly shocked, finding Jinny there well after curfew and then realizing he is standing there in his birthday suit.

Jimmy ran back to his bedroom, simultaneously screaming for Jamie. Poor Jinny has no idea what to do and quickly disappears before Jimmy has a chance to return with his pants on. After a brutal yelling match in which Jimmy accused Jamie of lying to him and breaking his cardinal rule and Jamie accused Jimmy of being a crazy, boring old man, it reached the point where Jamie yelled, "I want a round-the-clock staff in this house!" In reply, Jimmy yelled, "You can have your round-the-clock staff in another house—preferably as far away from me as possible!"

Jamie, who'd had enough by this point, was glad to be rid of Jimmy, and especially when she remembered her prenup agreement. You see, our Jimmy, while making sure not to do same prenup he made with Jenna, had been outsmarted by Jamie's lawyers. Among the endless pages of their prenup agreement, there was one clause he'd overlooked that said if Jimmy decided to divorce Jamie, he'd automatically forfeit their primary residence, wherever that might be. In this instance, it was their current residence overlooking Central Park, with a value of about forty-five million dollars.

The divorce was swift—owing either to good lawyer work or good prenup work or the mere fact that Jimmy and Jamie couldn't get away from each other fast enough. At any rate, it was done! Today, the ex-couple won't even say a polite "Hello" to each other at society functions. One must also wonder what other skeletons are hiding on the tenth, eleventh, and twelfth floors in a certain building gazing out over Central Park on the Upper East Side.

Oh, and Maid Jinny? She's now employed full-time with her own room in Jamie's three-floor penthouse, where she supervises a full-time household team of two maids and one butler.

To Jamie's way of thinking, who the hell needs a shrink when you can get therapy from your live-in and Eggs Benedict—all at the same time?

XOXO,
Guy Who Knows

The Prodigal Son

Hello, My Little Bees,

Spring is in full bloom in beautiful New York City.

As new leaves signal the season on the trees in Central Park, our Upper East Side ladies are also throwing themselves into their own renewal.

New hair, a new wardrobe, new shoes, a new degree of tanning (and some last-minute cosmetic touch ups), all just to have that natural, youthful glow that looks natural but costs the same as a small house in outer New Jersey. Nothing crazy, of course—mostly chemicals peels, fillers, Botox shots, eyelid lifts, neck touch-ups, and tummy tucks—you know, just the basics.

As the nights get warmer and the days grow longer, it could only mean one thing: wedding season is upon us! Time for families to put their best feet forward and show picture-perfect smiles as they attend million-dollar weddings at the Pierre, the Plaza, the New York Library—or, of course, the Hamptons. While they are there to share the joy of the newlyweds, enjoy fine dining, and dance the night away, there are other important agendas underneath the surface. One being business connections, and the other—far more important—that singles may mingle.

One of the most important things at any social gathering of this kind is for parents to showcase their young, bright, successful, and over-achieving children in society for the purpose of attracting suitable mates.

But what happens when one family has a less-than-desirable off-spring? Let us find out.

Please make the acquaintance of the Winefeld family. The mother, Karen, met dad Ken right after college. They married young, built a successful life, and had two kids. Their little princess, Kendell, is beautiful as rose and as well-guarded as that sweet girl in Beauty and the Beast. Ironically, while Kendell is the beauty, her brother Kevin is the beast. He's their first-born and unfortunately the outcast of the family.

As with royalty, the first-born Winefeld inherits the kingdom along with all its responsibilities. On the Upper East Side, boys are typically groomed to lead the way, to be the spitting image and continuation of their fathers' legacy. The problem in our story is that Kevin did not get the memo. It's not that Kevin didn't attend the finest schools. He was just too busy skipping classes to do recreational drugs. You see, Kevin was never projected to be an aerospace engineer or achieve world peace. However, he wasn't dumb either. But he did have an addiction problem—one that only got worse with time. What started with a little harmless green magic quickly escalated to far more serious and mind-altering drugs. On Madison Avenue, parents take pride in their offspring's success, even if there is none. For them, though, social acceptance is even more important than success. Sadly but often, it's the case that their little ones have financial resources that allow them to acquire drugs very easily. They consume them unsupervised and in peace while their parents are out and about—or not even. Often the parents simply choose to look the other way.

This particular writer witnessed for himself one "looking the other way" scenario in the Hamptons. In this instance, the fully aware parents allowed their seventeen-year-old kids and their friends to drink alcohol, smoke pot, and drive without a license along the roads of Easthampton—all in the name of Memorial Day weekend—without giving it a second thought. They themselves were too busy opening more bottles of rosé for their guests to intervene. But back to Kevin. As he grew older and his addiction pulled him into a downward spiral, his parents—like any good Upper East Siders—tried to sweep his issues under the rug. The problem, though, is that when you sweep too much under a rug, you start to get a lump. In Kevin's case, their decision to close their eyes and turn the other way wasn't wise. The lump in the carpet grew bigger and more noticeable every day.

As wedding season approached and invitations were mailed, Kendell and Kevin, as they are young adults, were also invited. After all, a match for each of them needed to be made, and there are few better places for matchmaking than the annual wedding circuit. On this Hamptons wedding weekend, our young Kevin had ingested a few too many of his personal party favors—enough to make a fool of himself. He then did some more, to the point that he overdosed. In the middle of a beautiful (and costly) custom wedding laser light show, one light began flashing that was not like the others. It was the telltale red light from the arriving police cars and ambulance. What was supposed to be a wonderful memory became a night of investigation and accusations. As we know, misery loves company, and it was soon learned that Kevin had not been enjoying his party favors alone.

When enough "donations" to police benevolence organizations had been made (along with a lot of other wheel-greasing we won't get into here), no other names of Kevin's party pals were officially tied to this little drama. The wedding, however, was ruined, and the reputation of the Winefeld family went right along with it. Now the Winefelds have one drug-addicted son and one beautiful and gracious daughter who has been marked as an "unsuitable" match for the high-society crowd.

Quickly after the wedding season ended, the Winefelds realized they were disgraced and had no choice but to flee their townhouse between Park and Madison for another set of apartments on the Upper West Side with stunning 360-degree views. Unlike where they came from, the Upper West Side houses a world where recreational drugs are less frowned upon—and sometimes even used legitimately for inspiration by the artistic community that largely resides there. Nonetheless, and to avoid any future embarrassment, Kevin was forced to attend one of the nation's best rehab facilities. He did the program and the whole thing was deemed a success.

However, upon returning, he was not the same Kevin. Before rehab, his parents had no delusions about him achieving greatness. Now his parents would be happy if he could hold down a job as mail carrier. Quiet sadly, his addiction, left untreated for so long, took its toll on his brain matter. While he can take care of himself, supervision should always be nearby.

Kendall, our rose, clever as she is beautiful, chose to attend a West Coast school, where luckily, she found a future husband from a West Coast family with no ties to Manhattan. The two decided on a small, family-oriented wedding with Malibu as the backdrop.

Personally, the only reason I go to weddings is for the drama. So I really don't understand what all the fuss is about. . .

XOXO,
Guy Who Knows

Anonymous

The Shoes Anecdote

Dear Followers,

If you've been reading diligently so far, I commend you! It is not easy reading about what is happening on the pavement of the Upper East Side—and even harder if you have to live it.

I do, however, want to give you another anecdote about life on Park Avenue.

The ladies of the Upper East Side are truly rare creatures who change outfits like a chameleon changes colors to suit its surroundings. And like the chameleon, no matter who you're putting on a show for, underneath it all you are who you are—and there's nothing you can do to change that.

As you know by now, being one of these ladies is a lot of work. They have their social gatherings, luncheons they must attend, clothes they must buy, shoes they must walk in until their feet blister and then they must run to their exclusive podiatrist to fix the damage they've done to themselves so they can again walk uncomfortably in twelve-inch heels.

I was always baffled by the extensive shoe collections of these ladies. And when you see their custom closets, with specialty compartments made just for shoes in an overall closet space big enough for a family of six, you are left without words.

One particular girl who plays the shoe game exquisitely is Farah Parker. When it comes to shoe collections, Farah doesn't miss a beat. She always has the best shoes. In her case, it's an addiction. Very rarely you will see Farah wearing the same heels twice! She is tall and slender, thanks to eight-inch heels and appetite suppressants. Farah has luxurious hair, thanks to $4,000 worth of hair extensions. She's always one of the chicest Upper East Siders because her style is edgy and unconventional. She never limits herself to Vogue's list of approved designers. She loves to find up-and-coming designers with unconventional silhouettes and uses safety pins for restraining her ample cleavage in shirts that leave extraordinarily little to the imagination. She has class and style and knows how to amp up every outfit to make herself stand out. One way she makes an unforgettable fashion impression is with her shoes. Cases of seeing Farah not in heels are exceedingly rare, like sightings of Big Foot. Though she may sport the most uncomfortable boots and shoes known to women anywhere on the planet, hers were always the hottest heels below 96th Street.

Farah's shoe collection was the envy of Madison Avenue. Hers is a unique collection not many women could wear—not only because of their heel height but also because they were mostly too edgy, something Cardi B might wear at the MTV Video Music Awards rather than a lady attending her annual hat luncheon at Central

Park's Conservatory Garden.

Farah knows the game and more, so she enjoys playing it. She's always by her husband's side, celebrating him as one of the Masters of the Universe. She's pretty, polite, educated, well-informed, and ranked quite high up on the social ladder. Farah is in fact everything an Upper East Side mom should be. On the inside, however, she's a party girl (formerly from upstate New York) who just wants to have fun!

One day while having lunch at Freds at Barneys, yours truly encountered Farah at midday, in broad daylight, and noticed her "sick" heels! Naturally, I raved about them, whereby she got a little too excited, raising her legs in the air in a perfect acrobatic move. Looking me dead in the eye, she agreed, "Aren't they sick?!" And indicating her legs, which were still aloft, she announced, "I love wearing them like this when my husband is fucking me!" A little confused—but certainly not shocked, I replied "Well, that's one way to get fucked." We chatted for few more minutes before kissing each other goodbye and planned to meet up soon. On the Upper East Side, you always make plans to "see each other soon." In many cases, it's the only way the conversation would ever end. Granted, the actual chance of your meeting up as promised are slim to none. Still, it is the polite thing to do!

Back to our story. You see, when I caught Farah lunching at Freds at Barneys, she wasn't really all there. In addition to her shoes, she has a fairy dust addiction, which for her is manageable at some level. It does not stop her from functioning and everyday socializing. On the sidewalks of Madison Avenue, as you know, we do not speak of such things. We never mention it when Farah comes back from the ladies' room with a cute white mustache—and not because she was sipping a skim cappuccino. Instead, we turn into chameleons, changing color to match our surroundings so everyone blends in quite naturally.

Move forward a few years. Farah got the help she needed to kick her addiction. As for her dependency on shoes, well, COVID-19 definitely put a damper on expanding her extensive collection. But worry not, bees. Farah is still as lovely and vibrant as ever, and just bought a new house with an even bigger shoe closet. What does that tell you? Like New York after COVID, Farah will be back bigger and better than ever!

And my own shoe collection, you ask? I really do prefer barefoot myself, which makes walking among the shadows so much easier.

XOXO,
Guy Who Knows

She Who Is Without Friends

Hello, Upper East Siders,

Hope your weekends were uplifting. Mine was eventful. As the sun rose high in the Hamptons, the mosquitoes swarmed in search of bluebloods. And my favorites—the bees—filled my cup with their luscious honey.

The Upper East Side is a collection of powerful women (in their minds) who form cliques and stick together. They are basically re-living their own high school years through the end of their lives, and they train their daughters to follow suit. How so? Well, usually, the moms sign their daughters up to attend the same summer camp they went to when they were girls. They also sign them up for some of the same camp courses they took, and sometimes even dress them the same. I've seen one-too-many old photos of mom in her camp days, resembling her daughter in the present and forcing me to chant the old anthem, "Oh my God, you two look just alike—so pretty!"

Yes, the ladies know their science. As germs do, they reproduce their daughters to be an exact copies of themselves. Thus, Madison Avenue produces generation after generation of ladies who look, think, and act the same. Nothing ever changes except their handbags. (Handbags are a whole religion in themselves, and one we will not be getting into today.)

One of the most important positive things these girls learn from their mothers is friendship—the value and power of loyalty, and how to stab a loyal friend in the back if need be.

So begins our story about Georgia.

Georgia is a typical Upper East Side mom. She's blonde, rich, and entitled, surrounded by many girlfriends who do everything together. They send their kids to the same school. They vacation together. In certain cases, they even share ex-husbands.

Georgia has one of the strongest girl cliques on Park Avenue. But whereas her clique all come from extremely rich families, were born and raised on the Upper East Side, attended high school and summer camp together, Georgia was a later addition. She married into the clique, to a New Yorker, and then moved right to the heart of the Upper East Side. Her charm, wit, and good looks were quickly noticed. Also, the fact she was awash in money made it easier for her to be befriended by that powerful, loyal clique.

Years later, as Georgia's husband eye wandered outside their two-story, six-bedroom mansion, she realized her time was up. She wanted to obtain a divorce while she was still a somewhat young and desirable woman. Unfortunately for her, her husband's wandering eye landed on one of her very best divorced friends in her girl clique.

Though Georgia thought it completely disloyal that her friend would take up with her estranged husband, her friend did not see it that way at all. And furthermore, instead of doing the girl clique friendly thing by explaining her position to Georgia, she quickly got the other girls on a conference call, and virtually overnight, poor Georgia was banned from their clique. And not only that. They banned her from their hair salon as well. All that transpired even before Georgia's divorce papers were drawn up!

On the Upper East Side, there is a clear and repetitive pattern of ladies forbidding other ladies from attending same places as they do, like dogs peeing on a tree to claim it. Lucky for us, Georgia is more resilient, and she basically did not give a fuck about any of these so-called friends.

So to recap. . . Georgia, a devoted mother of three and a loyal wife who grew up down South but moved to New York for her husband, got stripped of all her friends overnight because her husband took a fancy to one of those friends (who took a fancy to him, too). So if Georgia cannot get with the program and embrace their relationship, then she is a bad person. Makes perfect sense on Madison Avenue.

This was only the beginning of a very long gossip war on the Upper East Side, as Georgia was lucky enough to find another group of friends. That girl clique, while living on the UES, is a very interesting mix of working moms. One of them is one of the richest women on the planet. Another is a divorced foreigner with the attention span of cocker spaniel. A third is a complete whack job who goes around restaurants randomly asking other guests for a glass of water. When she is told by the guest that he is not a staff member, she then asks, "Well, can you ask someone for me?"

Poor Georgia's choice of friends is indeed lacking, because one-third of that group has decided she is not talking to Georgia anymore—the same one who also decided she is not talking with another member in the group. So basically, she's hogging the richest friend all for herself. Crazy.

During the lengthy divorce, Georgia's rich husband threw himself on the mercy of the court. He claimed that he was completely broke and without a dime to his name, which is a half-truth. He doesn't have one dime to his name. He has trillions of them in an untraceable offshore account. He further claimed that whatever money he had was invested in his company, which the books say is heavily in debt. After three years, Georgia decided to give up. She modestly requested only child support in the settlement, and thereby the divorce became final.

Luckily for her, Georgia got to keep some very expensive jewelry, which made it easier to keep up the appearance of the standard Upper East Side lifestyle.

Nowadays, Georgia's kids are socializing with different friends and attend different schools. They don't vacation with the rest of the flock, although her first-born does show signs of being the perfect

PTB (Princess To Be). And her mommy? She's dating an older man who seems promising. And what of her girl-clique friends? Well, she has learned one lesson. On the Upper East Side, there are no friends. Only power moves and alliances.

And me? I have many friends, of course—all of you!

XOXO,
Guy Who Knows

The Happy Couple

Dear Readers,

In the Hamptons, Memorial Day weekend marks the beginning of THE social season of the summer!

It's the season to let your hair down and spend time with family and loved ones—and not necessarily in that order.

The Hamptons is THE place to be if you are rich and famous. You know how they say Las Vegas is America's Playground? And they are right. Well, the Hamptons is America's richest playground. It has everything, including luxurious mansions, classic cars, lavish parties, girls- or guys-on-demand, drugs by prescription (or not), and service people to fulfill your every whim! From poolside massage to personal tennis lessons on your own private court to a personal chef cooking dinner for five, everything you want, everything private, nothing is unattainable. And the harder you play, the more popular you are!

Everyone wants to be in the Hamptons after the Memorial Day weekend. However, only the rich can experience the full effect. If you're not rich, you may still be lucky enough to participate, but you will never be fully immersed. Personally, I've found that when you've been to one of these Hamptons parties, you've been to them all. It's mainly about who spends the most money, but the outcome is always the same. Rich people clutching their drinks and doing drugs back in the private rooms of their mansions. They only pretend to enjoy the company they're in, faking smiles throughout the evening and repeating the same dull conversation to the same dull people from one party to the next.

It's almost tragic that those with the means to have a really good time are so bored and have such limited imaginations that their only excitement comes by using chemical (or sometimes naturally grown) aids for getting loose and have fun. Ultimately, the agenda of these parties is the same as any other social event on the Upper East Side—to strengthen your business connections and dominate the scene.

However, not everyone falls into the same pattern. Those who have been through the mill (and generally most of the older generation) know the sun and moon shine the same no matter what day it is. The cycle continues with no beginning or end, and the only way out is to forcibly break through the glass.

Please meet Joe and Jenna, your typical Upper East Side couple. J and J are a little past their prime years, but not old enough to retire to Palm Beach yet. Their kids are all grown, with families of their own, and aside from grandparents' weekend at summer camp and the recurring family reunions, the couple has absolutely no desire to stay home and babysit the young ones.

That does not mean Grandfather Joe doesn't enjoy spending time with those younger than him. In fact, Grandpa Joe does enjoy younger boys hanging around the house (particularly in their boxers)—in fact, a little too much. To satisfy his sweet tooth for eye candy, Gramps found the best next thing—a boy toy, who we will refer to here as Little Timmy.

Little Timmy is not little in age (and definitely not in other parts), but he does enjoy calling our grandfather "Daddy Joe."

Lovely.

Grandma Jenna doesn't know about Little Timmy, nor does she have time to care, what with getting her hair done three times a week and going on shopping sprees in which Daddy Joe supports her to the full extent of her credit card limit. Even if she reaches her limit—which often happens—there are always other cards ready to be swiped. While Jenna is out and about, Joe has ample time to play with his favorite boy and their favorite toys. . .

Up until recently, Joe and Jenna's permanent residence was their Fifth Avenue apartment. Not too long ago, they decided to move where the weather was warmer. Problematic for Little Timmy, whom was no longer in close proximity to Daddy Joe. But every problem has a solution, and Little Timmy began spending more time in Jet Blue airport lounges than the average flight attendant spends in the air. Yep, Timmy was commuting every week to visit his dear daddy.

When Spring had sprung, and it was time for J and J to move back to the Northeast, naturally the couple skipped over Manhattan and landed in Islip, driving directly from there to their summer home in Bridgehampton.

Recently, Daddy Joe did something he'd never done before: he brought his boy-toy to the Hamptons! Clearly, Daddy is one who wants to break the usual cycle of same parties, same people, same old boring conversations to spend more time with his lover. It is my personal knowledge—thanks to many bees I have buzzing around town—that Daddy decided to shop in one of his wife's favorite department stores, where he purchased a clothing item that wasn't his size or style but quite suitable for a twenty-some-thing-year-old man. This purchase was the clear declaration of a man wanting to get caught—or perhaps he was just taking notes from Caitlin Jenner's book on how to create a scandal. Why else would you tell the department store salesman to keep this little transaction quiet the next time he sees Daddy's wife—a regular VIP shopper!

One must wonder if Jenna is blind, or choosing to look the other way, or simply has an arrangement with Daddy to look the oth-er way that carries a cash dividend. As many of my girlfriends say, a woman always knows when her man cheats on her. She just weighs her options. Sometimes, she'd rather deal with an uncomfortable situation than be left completely alone.

In my opinion, if your man's heart belongs to someone else, you're already alone. But remember, on the Upper East Side, the worst things you can be are single, divorced, or broke. Clearly, Jenna is not ready for any of those.

Enjoy your summer and be careful where you shop. I just might be in the fitting room next to yours.

XOXO,
Guy Who Knows

Anonymous

A Tale of Two

Dear Readers,

My next story has everything you are craving: a male model, a lonely rich housewife, her closeted husband, and lots of betrayal! All happening against the background of Central Park during one warm summer.

Sasha arrives in America with nothing but the clothes on his back and a killer smile that would melt the ice off even the most prudent of ladies. His charm and good looks quickly earn him invitations to all the hottest parties in town, where he starts rubbing shoulders with the rich and powerful of New York City.

One night, he meets Lady Elodie—the epitome of wealth and deception. You see, she fled France because the government was after her for business misconduct. Elodie's husband, however, was not so lucky. He was caught and thrown in jail for life for his financial and other unmentionable crimes.

This husband still very much loves his wife and made sure to hide money in places the government cannot trace back to him. In America, that money helps Lady Elodie create a wonderfully comfortable life for herself as long as she stays within her budget. And what is her budget, you ask? For example, $200K a month for beauty products. They own buildings all over Manhattan, the income from which regularly pads their discreet bank account. She controls a network of fifteen service humans who cater to her every whim.

But Elodie was lonely and needed someone to fill the void in her heart (and other places). Luckily for her, she met Sasha, our gorgeous twenty-two-year-old model with the body of Zeus and the brain of an antelope. They sure did have fun together, traveling all over the world except for France, where she was a wanted woman. She showered Sasha with lavish gifts like a brand-new Corvette. She took him to every luxurious party on her calendar—somewhere not even the richest on Park Avenue were allowed in.

The fairy tale was almost complete if not for one tiny problem: Sasha was gay.

He began as a stranger to the underbelly of gay New York, closeted men's private clubs where one can only join if one is prominent in his field and has been invited into the club by one of its other members—or alternately, if you have a stunning body and come as the guest of a current club member.

One night at the men's club, Sasha met William—a married contractor with two kids who built half of New York. The two hit it off right away and started having an affair.

Elodie knew nothing of Sasha's straying, except that her lover often disappearing for days at a time on "photo shoots"—trips from which there were never any photos to be seen and after which Sasha seemed less inclined to ravish her in the ways she was used to. William had an extensive investment portfolio and could very easily fly under the radar. At one of his properties, William showed Sasha the ropes—quite literally. In fact, those rope marks on Sasha's arms (and probably other places) were the talk of the party at Elodie's fiftieth birthday extravaganza.

One night, Elodie's suspicions finally got the better of her and she confronted Sasha. While he did not disclose the real reason for his frequent absences, he did leave the very next day—along with a million dollars' worth of her jewelry, which enabled him to stay under the radar himself for several months. All the while, Elodie was offering a substantial reward up and down Madison Avenue to anyone who caught sight of Sasha and her gems and called her right away!

No one knows what happened during those three months, but one day, Sasha emerged out of the blue as a broker for a high-end real estate firm (nothing under twenty million dollars, please), with a business card and everything! Anyone doing a quick online search of his name will instantly see the company staff picture, including Sasha. And who do you suppose is standing next to him in that photo, shoulder to shoulder? You guessed it—William!

Apparently in those three months, William was busy divorcing his wife, leaving her nothing but the house and the two kids while he started raising a "son" of his own (less than half his age, by the way).

Wherever you see Sasha today, you also see William—but as a "colleague." The story goes on, with new pictures emerging every quarter as the buzzing continues.

I think I will attend Sasha's next private showing and see if I can get my shoulder rubbed. I'll be sure to bring my rope.

XOXO,
Guy Who Knows

Fairy Tale Gone Wrong
THE LILY NEWCASTLE STORY

Dear Readers,

WARNING: The following is a tragic story without a happy ending. Please proceed with caution.

We all know the classic fairy tales where boy meets girl, girl falls in love with the boy, and they live happily ever after. But what is "happily ever after"? Does it really exist? Not in Lily Newcastle's case.

Her story starts like all others. A girl comes from the slums, finds her king, falls in love, becomes rich, provides heirs for the king, and then finds out that real-life stories are not written by Disney. If you do not like sad endings, stop reading now!

Name:	Lily Newcastle
Occupation:	None
Status:	Married to a husband who cannot stand her
Kids:	Six

Our story begins when Lily moves from the slums of the countryside to the big city for "work" in real estate. By "work," we mean her principal task is to find a suitable guy to marry. On the Upper East Side, love has no room when planning one's future. Love has been replaced with a series of boxes for a woman to check. If a suitor gets checks in all her boxes, fulfilling all her requirements, she can declare that they are in love and begin her wedding day countdown.

Such was Lily's case. She met a handsome guy—young, successful, and from a good family. He was practically royalty. She, on the other hand, was poor, young, and skinny, with exotic notes to her appearance. Still, she was well-mannered and knew how to play the game, dress up, laugh at his jokes even if he was not so funny, and adopt the necessary social graces in order to survive among the wealthy. It did not take our couple long to marry and grace the private school sector with six boys. As we know on the Upper East Side, the more kids you have, the richer you are.

When couples have nothing in common and come from a completely different backgrounds, it can be a hit or miss. In Lily's case, it was a big MISS.

Rumors circulated that Lily's husband could not stand her, that he felt she was nothing more than a womb to him and the caretaker of his army of boys. With a personal assistant, two drivers, a chef, a personal trainer, two housekeeping ladies, three nannies, and an after-school tutor for each child, Lily still finds herself exhausted. In a fully staffed home like hers, one might think she has time for herself—and she does, PLENTY of it. However, in her mind, she is a super-busy working mom who has no time do anything (even though she has time to visit her favorite beauty salon for her daily blowout right after her daily spin class and before her daily lunch with the girls followed by daily visits to a rotating list of her favorite shops). With that lifestyle, I would be exhausted too!

Oh, another thing. A source very close to the family mentioned to me that Lily awakens every morning forty-five minutes before her husband to get out her cosmetics so he will never ever see her without makeup! Her signature look is taking one eye shadow color from the palette in her compact, covering her lids in that color for days on end until there's nothing left of that particular shade and then moving on to the next.

Now a woman with such a lavish lifestyle and no time on her hands would probably bear many interesting topics for conversation, right? WRONG. The only subject on Lily's lips is the fact that her husband hates her, pays no attention to her, and never shows her an ounce of love or appreciation. Actually, this is incredibly sad, because I believe we all deserve to live with people who love and admire us. But Lily believes in the finer things in life—first-class airfare and having a black American Express card at her disposal, no matter how miserable she is.

One of the boys' ex-tutors revealed to me that the tutor is now only allowed to be home when Dad is not. It just so happened that one time, Dad walked in earlier than expected to find the tutor there. Lily immediately terminated the tutoring session and asked this tutor to leave right away. Was Lily afraid that our boy's tutor, a gorgeous former pageant runner-up, would steal her husband's attention and then his heart? Maybe.

Please make no mistake. Lily's husband, the father of her children, is a very loving, well-educated man from a good family and is pleasant to be around! What's the problem then, you ask? I will leave it to you to decide.

As advertised, this fairy tale has no happy ending. Lily continues her daily routine while the kids are in school, the staff are fully engaged, and no one pays her any attention whatsoever.

I cannot wait to squeal and reveal that a certain UES dad happens to be having a secret romance with a handsome twenty-two-year-old blonde who also knows how to play the game.

XOXO,
Guy Who Knows

Cinderella & The Sugar Daddy

Dear Readers,

It is another summer day on the Upper East Side, and we know that can only mean one thing: a long line of bored doormen in the buildings along Park Avenue. No one is there to open a door for. Our beloved ladies, along with their staff and fancy cars, are soaking up sun in fairytale castles out in the Hamptons. Their kids are soaking up mud and sweat at their favorite summer camps.

Oh yes, the summer camps! Eight weeks out of the year that parents will give their right arms (and a yearly salary for the average Joe) to send their little ones away so parents can play uninterrupted with their own toys. On the Upper East Side, a parent is never truly free until their young adult reaches their eighteenth birthday. While moms tend to cling even more to their offspring, dads are ready and willing to part ways with a firm handshake, a bit of fatherly advice, and, of course, handing them their own Platinum American Express cards.

In certain cases, moms are so concerned with their offspring's lives that they completely forget to attend to their husbands' needs. This never ends well, especially for the wife. Her spousal neglect could lead to her husband either having an affair or choosing an altogether different life.

Meet Jacob.

Jacob is a successful businessman of Middle Eastern origins. He moved to New York at a very young age with a heartfelt desire to live the American Dream. Along the way, he met a beautiful girl, married her, and had three wonderful children.

Jacob went into the real estate business at an early age. As his family grew, so did his net worth. After a few years, he had become a multi-millionaire. He and his wife Debra raised their kids to perfection. They attended good schools and were brought up with solid values. While they attended camps, they were only day camps—perhaps because the family did not live on the Upper East Side but in one of the lesser boroughs. Perhaps Jacob cared more about having nightly dinners with his family than the UES dads. Family meant the world to him.

During the day, Jacob worked so he could take care of his family. At night, he wanted to enjoy the rewards of his labors—a desire his wife did not share. While Jacob liked to dine out, party, dance, and mingle, Rebecca only wanted to lounge on the sofa and watch Oprah and her favorite soaps. Tragic.

By now, all Jacob's kids had reached the age of eighteen. He'd done his best to teach them the value of family. He taught them everything he could up to this point, and it was time to teach them one more lesson: how to put yourself first and be happy! Within three months, Jacob divorced Rebecca. He gave her everything she wanted in the settlement. The couple parted ways, with Jacob heading toward a bright, unknown future.

In his mid-fifties and now a bachelor, Jacob was in his glory years. He purchased the perfect bachelor pad on the borderline between the Upper East Side and Midtown East with a panoramic view of the city. With his new bachelor friends, Jacob went out every night—partying, womanizing, drinking, smoking, doing every drug on the market, and getting himself the most expensive call girls in New York. There is not one high-end madam's black book in the city that Jacob's name and phone number do not appear in. While there is much I could tell you about his newfound youth, this is not our story.

Now that you have the background, we can start.

One day while out on the town, Jacob met Kelli, the perfect young woman, also of Middle Eastern descent. She was in her late twenties, while he was pushing sixty. The two made an instant connection! They were both from the same country and spoke the same language. There was no culture gap, and they felt so comfortable with each other that they began dating immediately.

During their dating, Jacob showered Kelli with extravagant gifts and took her to the hottest places, where she got to rub shoulders with New York's rich and famous. He gave her the taste of a life she'd never known. And as we know, money is like drugs. It can be very addicting, and you always want more.

The problem was that Kelli wanted to secure this moneyed future for herself. Though she and Jacob were dating, Jacob was far from monogamous. He did not quit his lavish bachelor nights. In fact, he started bankrolling exclusive, ultra-private orgies that took place in a certain Soho loft.

Kelli knew all about Jacob's drug-filled nights and orgies. She knew that she was not the only girl in his life and that she wasn't the only woman he was romantically involved with. However, Jacob's list of bed partners had gotten longer than the Brooklyn Bridge. What could Kelli do? She had developed a taste for Jacob's extravagant lifestyle. In fact, it was more like a craving. She also knew that in her line of work, to live like she lived when she was with Jacob was an impossible dream.

Torn between her desire to get married and have a baby and her desire to be rich, Kelli choose the later. However, it is the Upper East Side, and we do love a good business arrangement.

Jacob offered Kelli the life she wanted—unlimited travel, clothes, bags, shoes, funds, and even support for her family in exchange for two things. First, no marriage. Jacob made it clear they will NEVER EVER be wed. Second, as long as she remained in this relationship, she could not have a baby. Jacob should always be her priority.

In addition to these two conditions, Jacob made it clear he was not about to stop using drugs or quit his orgies. Rather, he wanted Kelly to join him. Just like Arielle in The Little Mermaid who sold her voice to the evil sea witch to exchange her mermaid's tail for legs—Kelli signed away her soul in exchange for a piece of Jacob's wealth.

You can quit almost every drug in the world, but you cannot quit being rich.

Overnight, Kelli quit her job and was seen touring the floors of Barney's with a personal shopper, filling bags on each floor she visited. A driver waited outside to whisk her over to Hermès, where she skipped the waiting line and purchased one of their rare and iconic ostrich skin bags, the definitive UES status symbol. That became Kelli's daily routine. She woke up each morning to nourish her soul in shopping so she could hand it over to the Devil at night and be used as he pleased—all in the name being able to afford high fashion.

Years passed, and Jacob aged. Kelli was not as hot as when they first met either. Jacob slowed his lifestyle down. No more drugs or orgies. But there were still strange partners visiting their shared bed more than once a week.

One morning, Kelli took a long, hard look at herself and did not like what she saw underneath the thousand-dollar skin creams and makeup. She saw a girl who had given up her dream of becoming a mother and had nothing to show for it! Nothing was in her name—not the houses, nor the jewelry nor the cars. They were not married, so she was entitled to nothing if she left the relationship. Jacob, however, loved Kelli very much. They had stayed together for almost twenty years, and she had remained beside him through it all. Kelli hoped that would count for something.

When she finally told Jacob she wanted to have a baby, Jacob was gracious and understanding. He told her he would support her decision, and even finance it for her—meaning he would pay for the sperm donor (because he didn't want any more kids of his own), and he would pay for all her medical needs. However, Kelli had to leave before the baby arrived. Now more than seventy years old, Jacob had no intention of being a father again. The only "daddy" he desired to be was someone's Sugar Daddy.

At length, Kelli decided that no money in the world could stop her from fulfilling her destiny. She agreed to leave Jacob before the baby arrived. During the entire process of getting pregnant and her pregnancy, Kelli was nervous and worried. How would she manage being poor again?? Her anxiety was so great that she lost all her hair and did not leave the house. The sand in her hourglass had almost run out. She found an apartment and prepared to move. Jacob allowed her to take whatever she wanted with her and even offered financial support to start out her new life right. But as Kelli's due date approached, Jacob had a surprising change of heart. He realized that not everything in life is a business arrangement—even in our little nation of the Upper East Side. Perhaps it was due to their cultural kinship. Whatever his reason, he decided to hang onto Kelli and her baby and raise the child as his own.

Kelli understood everything in life happens the way it should, and love could indeed triumph over everything—including money. Who said fairy tales don't exist today? This particular princess may not have kissed the frog who became a handsome prince. But she found the goose who lays the golden eggs.

And for me? The only orgy I'm allowing myself is with a quart of Ben & Jerry's.

XOXO,
Guy Who Knows

Persona Non Grata

My Dear Nosey-Rosies,

It is a splendid afternoon in New York City. Madison Avenue just put out her display of upcoming Fall fashions—like freshly bloomed flowers on a field of green. The bees are flying in to be first at sucking all the honey they can, leaving the stores owners well padded. This is a very common practice on the Upper East Side. You attend the fashion show, then rush over to purchase everything you can. Then you throw a party so you can wear your fashion and rock you frock like a cock on a rock, so to speak.

One particular Bee, however, will not be participating in this ritual anytime soon.

Do you remember Elbit, son of Mr. and Mrs. Rose, aka The Phone Whisperer?

Remember how I talked about his off-hour whereabouts, while his lovely trophy wife stayed behind? Well, his wife's name is Diana. And let me tell you, she is not a princess.

Diana met Elbit after the two had already graduated from college and were well into their lives as young adults. He was already heir to the family business and its fortune. She came from a comfortably well-off family—but not nearly as comfortable as the Roses. Diana knew the rules: be pretty, polite, blend into the background, never speak your opinion, and do not draw attention to yourself.

After they got married, the game advanced, but the rules stayed the same. Diana still had to do everything as before, but now, she also had to produce babies and raise them—or more correctly hire an army of nannies to help her handle one kid and oversee the household staff to make a warm, pleasant habitat for Hubby.

As I mentioned before, Elbit saw Diana as his trophy wife. Though he too had to play the game of getting married and having family, he was not bound by any rules. Elbit liked his single life before he met Diana. Being young, handsome, and wildly rich in Manhattan is the ultimate fantasy for many people, including Elbit. He spent his nights with different women all over town. While he never took another woman to a formal event or a top-notch restaurant, he did barhop all over Manhattan with different women on his arm—some for fun, and some he paid for. And YES, Elbit did like to stay happy at all times, particularly with alcohol and other forms of happiness that are not sold at your local Duane Reade. Diana knew all about her husband's sexcapades, but she chose to turn a blind eye to his wanderings and instead enjoyed the perks of being a Rose family member. She had an account with every high-end store and service provider in Manhattan and East Hampton. Everywhere she went, they knew who she was and never bothered to ask her for payment—whether she was getting her highlights at Freda Hazan or shopping for evening wear at Oscar De Le Renta. She simply came in and left. Her bill was always settled and her goods delivered to their apartment, neatly placed in her 1,000-square-feet walk-in closet by a member of her household staff.

There was, however, one issue. As you should know by now, on the Upper East Side, one must flaunt one's wealth, but in a classy (not a tacky) way. And how do we that? Answer: by having large families. The UES rule of thumb is four kids if you're a multi-millionaire. If you have five kids, well, then money is nothing but a piece of paper for you. Unfortunately for our happy little couple, Elbit and Diana had a hard time conceiving the first time, and even more so the second. One could blame it on Elbit's overuse of fairy dust mixed with nonprescription pills which he slips down his throat with a shot of Tequila. Or one could presume that his sperm count is so low you can count them on one hand. But no one is to know.

That little pickle (pun intended) was a real issue for the elder Roses. They wanted more grandkids, and Elbit wanted to make them and Diana happy. As I said, she could not care less about her husband's nighttime activities as long as she got everything she wanted and then some. Like most failed and unproductive business arrangements, someone had to be the blamed and take the fall. In this case, it was Diana.

Elbit decided he want to divorce her, claiming to inner circles that she was unable to get pregnant and provide him with the necessary heirs. Immediately, the entire family stood solidly behind El-bit. Overnight, Diana was cast out and became persona non grata on the Upper East Side!

Doors to her hair salon, her doctor's office, and all the stores she had ever loved were now shut in her face! The Roses gave instructions everywhere that Diana no longer had use of the family accounts. They went so far as to tell the owners that if they preferred Diana's business over theirs, even if she paid them from her own pocket, then the Roses would take their business elsewhere. Trust me, no one wants that! Their budget, like their bank accounts, knows no limits. Furthermore, the Roses went one step further, spreading the rumor all of over Madison Avenue that Diana had a secret affair outside of wedlock and thereby destroyed the family!! Like Princess Diana (but not as tragic), our Diana's life had become a mess because of an overbearing, control-freak family and a lying, cheating husband.

Poor Diana had to leave Manhattan, relinquish her "Rose" last name, and raise their son in Connecticut. Make no mistake, the house she lives in was bought and paid for by the Roses, and her monthly alimony is substantial enough to fund a small island. After all, Diana is still in charge of raising their first-born, who could one day be heir to the Rose dynasty.

Elbit still stayed in the picture, seeing his son on alternate weekends and holidays. He never got married again, and in fact attended rehab twice—not here in America, where someone might find out. He did his rehab in a private, ultra-exclusive facility in Europe on the cusp of the Mediterranean.

What Elbit and the Roses are forgetting is that all secrets are bound to see the light of day, and I am nothing but a humble writer who enjoys opening doors and letting the light come in.

XOXO,
Guy Who Knows

Anonymous

The AA Member

My Dear Readers,

It's time to wake up, Upper East Siders! Drink your black coffee and take two Advil to nourish your hangover—the results of your indulging last night at Ms. Season's over-the-top, "Let me show you how rich I am," "My boyfriend will never marry me" fortieth birthday party.

As I said before, if you been to one party in the Hamptons, you've been to them all. All are opportunities to drink your night away, make bad choices, spill some secrets, cause a commotion, and, of course, receive gossip topics for the following week—all while your kids are at sleep-away camp and think you are home having salad for dinner, watching your favorite show, and going to sleep by 9:00 p.m.

There are, however, those among us who choose not to participate in these sorts of parties because they know they can't be trusted with themselves.

Acquaint yourself with Mrs. Rena Cohn, the lovely mother of two future violinists and wife of Baron Cohn, a real estate developer who since 1990 built Downtown NYC almost single-handedly and is heir to a multi-billion-dollar family fortune.

Rena is knowing for not understanding what a watch is for. Most of us understand it tells times and indicates when we have to be at our appointments. For Rena, however, it is a distraction. In her mind, just because her watch says it's noon and she has a lunch scheduled at that hour doesn't mean she can't show up at 1:00 p.m. Obviously, the world must move according to her time and not the other way around. Time tracking is something that stresses her out.

Makes sense in her world.

Rena was born and raised here—a true New Yorker. And while she came from a comfortably well-off family, she was never rich. That is, until she met and married Baron, and her whole life changed. Just as the butterfly begins its life cycle as a worm, shields itself inside a cocoon, and then emerges at the beautiful butterfly, so it was with Rena. She started as an ordinary person, got cocooned by an extremely wealthy family, and emerged as an Upper East Side lady and all that entails. The problem was that Rena was ill-prepared for such a demanding life. She had to juggle being a stay-at-home mom with a staff of three with caring for her husband and mothering two destined-to-be-overachieving girls. It proved to be a challenge she simply could not handle. Combined that with her inability to track time and be where she should be when need be and you have a recipe for disaster!

What's a girl to do when dealing with so much stress? One of the coping mechanisms of Upper East Side ladies is to stop eating and start drink heavily—so heavily that you pass out on the floor during a normal dress fitting for you daughter's graduation at a major designer (#gossipmagazine). Rena couldn't wake up in the mornings and function as a human being anymore. She knew she was in a bad spot and her loving husband agreed.

Not to worry, though. On Madison Avenue, there are hush-hush solutions for everything. After a quick two-month visit during the perfect time—the summer months—while claiming they were in Europe, Baron and the girls spent time at a secluded farm on the West Coast, while Mommy Dear spent time at a rehab facility in the center of our great country.

Within these months, Rena managed to kick her addiction completely to the curb (good for her!) and emerged as a vital member of society instead of drinking her day away. She decided to fill her daily calendar with every distraction possible to avoid even thinking of drinking. Instead, she indulged herself in other less dangerous addictions such as getting her hair done, shopping, and, of course, daily attendance at her local AA meeting right here on Madison Avenue.

Yes, Madison Avenue has its one chapter of Alcoholics Anonymous, but this is not public information. It's actually quite smart, as this facility (the location I will keep to myself) is the perfect hiding place. I guess their Chanel sunglasses shade our UES ladies so well that they can't even see what's right under their bought-

and-paid-for noses (and boobs).

Rena attends her AA meetings laden with shopping bags and marks on her calendar "doctor's appointment" for these sessions.

Today, Rena has luckily found her calling in the philanthropic arts. While she attends many charity luncheon in New York and the Hamptons, she always stays clear of the bar and limits her attendance at any event if her husband is not nearby. She extends her generosity to her family, although one might claim that her family is more demanding than gracefully accepting of her favor. But that's none of our business.

What's family for, if not to milk their cash cow for all you can get? Oh, and one more thing. Dear Rena didn't quite kick all her toxins to the curb. If as you stroll on the side streets of the Upper East Side between Madison and 5th Avenues and spot someone in hiding, sneaking a drag of cig while holding multiple shopping bags of couture fashion, please stop and say hi to Rena. The mortified look on her face will give you just enough to keep your day rolling.

XOXO,
Guy Who Knows

Girl Gone Wild, Part II

Dear Bees,

Sometimes it is great to be me! Something wonderful just happened, and I couldn't think of a better way to share my good fortune than writing to tell you all about it. You judge for yourself.

It was a casual late Thursday evening, and I was sitting down to watch The Real Housewives of Beverly Hills. The drama, courtesy of host and puppeteer Andy Cohen, was just amping up when my phone rang unexpectedly. Who could be calling at this ungodly hour? I was not accustomed to taking calls that late. Initially, I assumed it must be bad news. However, my fears were completely vaporized when I read the caller ID. It was one of my favorite buzzing bees on the Upper East Side!—someone who has UES ladies eating out of his hand. I knew he called bearing gifts, and true to form, he did not disappoint.

Do you remember Lorelai? What about Blondie? If you don't, you clearly haven't been keeping up, and you are missing out!

Lorelai and Blondie used to be the best of friends, which in itself is odd. Lorelai does not come from money, while all Blondie knows is money. Stranger friendships have happened. But for these two, the writing was on the wall from the very start.

They met in New York a few years back through a mutual friend. Immediately, the two hit it off based on common interests, namely, older men and lots of alcohol. Lorelai and Blondie became like sisters, practically inseparable. They used to go out all the time and frequently set up play dates for their kids. Blondie, being the good loyal friend that she is, even helped Lorelai get an apartment when her "sister" was down on her luck.

Those who are keeping up will recall that Lorelai became broke at some point and could no longer afford her tiny Upper East Side apartment. So what did she do? She left town, hoping to find a pot of money somewhere warm. And who was left on the hook for said apartment? You are correct: Blondie! Lorelai had used her as a guarantor on her lease. Sadly, on Madison Avenue, there are no real friendships, only arrangements—and most likely one person or the other always gets screwed (and not in the way they might like). The screw-ee, in our case, was dear sweet Blondie.

Lorelai's leaving town caused everything to go sour between the two. Their friendship went "Poof!" up in smoke. With Lorelai out of the scene and Blondie left in her dust to pick up the pieces, you might think things would just die down. But apparently, geographic distance did nothing to calm the waters between these two former sisters. Their feud was about to creep back over state lines and then blow back into town with a vengeance. Listen to what happened.

Back to my precious bee on the phone, who was privy to a call within the New York DA's office—a crime investigation involving two women, coincidentally Lorelai and Blondie.

It appears that Lorelai is back in town and nesting on the Upper East Side. Her new UES flat was provided by a certain gentleman who recently left his wife in exchange for visitation rights with Lorelai, if you know what I mean. Lorelai's reappearance made Blondie furious, as she is still on the hook for $75K in back rent for the girl's previous apartment and has been chasing her down to collect the money ever since!

Blondie embarked on a campaign to ruin Lorelai's life completely. She called everyone she knew and spread less-than-nice words about Lorelai to whoever would pick up the phone. If that wasn't enough, according to my source, she even threatened Lorelai's life. While I find this a little hard to believe, Upper East Siders are certainly unbalanced enough to make such threats, thanks to their liberal use of prescription medications. However, they typically are not violent. And we must remember that Lorelai is an outsider and does not feel compelled to play the game according to Madison Avenue rules.

Lorelai could not remain silent. In response to Blondie's threat, she picked up her own phone, called a certain gentleman of her acquaintance, and had Blondie arrested! Now you must understand Blondie is not your typical soccer mom. She is multi-millionairess, practically royalty. Being escorted from her Park Avenue building in chains with a less-than-perfect blowout is not something you see every day.

Now that, my darlings, could only mean one thing on the Upper East Side: WAR. And not only that, but it also appears that Blondie, courtesy of a restraining order, must now stay away from Lorelai by at least two hundred feet! To twist the dagger more deeply in Blondie's back, Lorelai had strolled along Madison Avenue and established herself as a client at all of Blondie's favorite hangouts. Now Blondie can no longer visit any of those places while Lorelai is in residence without breaking the law. Blondie has been effectively bumped and must now get her manicures over on Lexington. Sad.

I seriously doubt this will be the end of it. You can trust that my ears and eyes are open, and I will be writing to you as soon as I know more.

XOXO,
Guy Who Knows

From China With Love

Dear Readers,

You better set your coffee down, shut the door, and put your phone on Do Not Disturb for this one.

So far, we have met so many wonderful ladies living along the coveted avenues of the Upper East Side. But now, it's time to introduce you to a foreign figure—one for the books.

If you've been around the block, you know who I am referring to. The only question is how much you know.

Meet Ming Lee.

Beautiful, tall Asian lady with skin as white as snow and fiery red hair. She is well into her fifties now and retired.

"Retired from what?" you are asking. I'll explain.

Ming Lee was first discovered back when she was working the malls in China. The man who discovered her back in the eighties was a charming New York legend—we'll call him Ziggy. Ziggy saw Ming Lee and knew right away that a girl like her should not be standing and selling souvenirs to passing tourists. He knew he could use her long skinny figure and beautiful face to advance both their careers.

True, she didn't have a career yet. But that was about to change. Ming Lee was swept off her feet when Ziggy told her all about the American Dream and what the future had in store. This future was ready and waiting for her. All she had to do was sign her soul away to the Devil. It took less than six months, and Ming Lee's immigration paperwork was in order. Her fairytale life—a girl overcoming poverty, stress, and misery to become a beautiful princess—was about to come true. She was flown first-class to JFK, where a limousine with a glass of champagne was waiting for her. From there, it was straight to her suite at a luxurious Midtown hotel. Ziggy was waiting to greet her with a big smile, a bear hug, and a stiff one (and I am not referring to a cocktail).

Ming Lee was confused. Jet lagged, possibly slightly drugged, her first-time seeing New York City (and so far, only through a car window), arriving at one of New York's most luxurious hotels, she did not know what to do with the situation unfolding before her. Not particularly a gentleman, Ziggy bluntly explained to Ming Lee that this was the way things were done in America. He'd paid everything for her to come to New York. Before he could strut her stuff down Fashion Avenue, he needed to make sure she had what it takes to succeed in this business (his words, not mine).

There is no way to sugar coat it. Ming Lee was taken advantage of by a rich, powerful guy. This was before social media and the #MeToo movement. Ziggy told Ming Lee she must understand that everyone goes through this. It was essential that she complied in order to have a successful career.

The twist in the story is that Ming Lee never made it to Fashion Avenue. In fact, she never felt victimized by what had happened to her with Ziggy. Rather, she understood through that experience the power she held within herself. Now, she wasn't a virgin when she first met Ziggy, and she definitely wasn't one when she arrived in NYC. However, her comfort level with the situation did make Ziggy understand that her future might be brighter than he imagined.

As he promised, Ziggy introduced Ming Lee to all the agencies, producers, photographers, and artistic people in New York. She quickly caught everyone's attention. Ming Lee was confident and willing to do whatever it took to never again be without money. Every audition Ming Lee went on was in fact a private audition, usually taking place in a private suit or residence outside of the city.

Ming Lee became a brand name among the rich, powerful men of the city. She soon understood that to really move up the ladder, she needed to be more than just beautiful face. She would need to be a vital part of elite society to further her agenda. Modeling, she quickly understood, was not for her. With her killer body and other skills, she managed to get a group of men to secure her a high position at an institute of culture, where she could help throw lavish parties, bring in big donors, and as they say, "kill two birds with one stone."

One bird was raising money to serve the needy, which is always a good thing in New York. The other was to expand her social connections and her client base.

If you haven't figured it by now, Ming Lee was a call girl—but not just any call girl. She was the highest paid, most in-demand, and most skillful call girl in all of New York City. It was said that to spend a night with Ming Lee cost nothing short of $5000. This fee assured her that she wouldn't have to worry about money or work her ass off (pun intended) for everyone who wanted her services. Only the best of the best would get that privilege.

Her striking look made her popular among designers and fashion moguls. She was now invited to every fashion show in New York, where she sat front row center with her big Gucci sunglasses, dressed in haute couture. Ming Lee appeared in every social magazine, thanks to the paparazzi who couldn't get enough of her. Now that she had caught the public eye, the ladies of the Upper East Side began noticing her too, and quickly lined up to befriend her. Ming was happy to dip her feet into that pool.

She'd seen rich people and understood the wealth this country had to offer her. But now she also understood how there is one neighborhood in the world where money is nothing but mere paper. By accessing the neighborhood and befriending the Madison Avenue ladies, she also befriended their husbands—and she was a woman with a mission. Having this newfound source of endless opportunities, she had men buying her apartments (yes, not one but two!) on the Upper East Side. By now, a night with Ming Lee was said to cost more than $20K!

This fairy tale just wouldn't be complete without at least one villain. And on Madison Avenue, there is never just one. Villains here almost always come in groups. We already know that when these ladies have their minds set on bringing someone down, it's not even a challenge for them—just an ordinary Tuesday.

One woman in particularly—we'll call her Marla—decided to learn more about Ming Lee. How did she do it? Simple. She had her over for a social lunch so they get better acquainted. Ming Lee knew she had to comply, as Marla was a high-ranking socialite with ties to every organization in New York. Her last name was on more NYC buildings than Con Edison's. Luckily for Ming, the lunch went well, and she didn't disclose too much of herself to Marla. Marla, however, got exactly what she needed—just enough to start a private investigation. The investigation was fruitless. Marla only found out Ming Lee wasn't born in country she said she was from, and that she had no relatives there either. All the other info she gave Marla came back false. There was no history on Ming Lee to be found anywhere. It was as if she had never existed before she arrived in New York.

That only made Marla angrier. She decided that if her first investigator couldn't find the information she wanted, someone else would. And thanks to her powerful connections, the authorities decided to look into Ming Lee's past. And boy oh boy, the things they found...

One morning, Ming Lee heard a knock on the front door of her newest and most luxurious apartment yet. Instantly she thought, "How is it possible that, in a building with a doorman where every guest must be announced, can there be someone knocking on my door?" And who do you think was in fact knocking on her door?

Well, my Rosie Nosies, unfortunately, someone is knocking on my own door, and I must go see who it is. Not to worry. I'll be back before you know it, and I'll explain to you in detail who was knocking on Ming Lee's door. A little hint: it wasn't her dry cleaner.

XOXO,
Guy Who Knows

And Now, When All is
Said and Done

Well, hello there,

Did you enjoy all of that? How do you feel now? Informed? Educated? Amused? Maybe you feel like you need a shower after rolling in the mud? Or perhaps you're sitting there in disbelief that these are actually real people.

So what did we learn here?

A lady with an affection for cows. A lady who threw her dog a million-dollar birthday party. A modern day Upper East Side princess who lives in a thunder dome. A woman and her husband who think they're royalty. We met women with addiction problems, men problems, and the far more serious and disturbing, pooping problems, as in the case of Megan Long.

We now understand the value of friendship, from Georgia and her group of girlfriends who decided to turn on Georgia because one of the inner circle girls began dating Georgia's soon-to-be ex-husband—and of course Georgia is the villain in their eyes. Who can forget Blondie and Lorelai, the two best friends who are now working out their differences downtown at the district attorney's office?

The Madison Avenue beauty salon is the new religion, as we saw on many occasions—such as the case of Mrs. Dime and Mindi Arch and even more in Pipa's case, who refused to give birth before getting her vagina waxed clean! Appearance is everything on Madison Avenue. Even if they all look the same, that's fine—as long as they can throw lavish parties in their summer Hamptons homes, be around the same people, and have same dull conversation over and over again.

We now know the Upper East Side ladies will stop at nothing. They will fly in their private staff (and under secrecy if need be), build new buildings to keep their sons enrolled in private schools, pay people to spy for them, and win lawsuits in courts to keep their multi-million-dollar houses overlooking Central Park.

We also had stories about some men: a cheating man, a lying man, a gay man, a man who liked to be alone, a man who wanted to be a bachelor forever. The one thing all these men have in common is that they are all married to women who look the other way—in most cases just to keep their wallets well padded.

Yes, it was a lot to absorb. But let's admit it, we had fun doing so. These ladies provide more fantastic stories than any I could have imagined in my weird little head. And trust me when I tell you, this is just the tip of the Upper East Side iceberg! There are so many ladies out there who continue to strut their stuff and gossip their stories all the way to my perky ears. Wait till you read Part II. I, of course, will continue do what I do best. I'll be the fly on the wall, or the person sitting right in the middle of it, stirring the conversation and giving all the skeletons air to breathe.

Yes, you know these ladies. You've read about some of them. Some of them you've even met in person. A couple have been the subject of documentary films!

Who are they?

That's one secret I'll never tell.

XOXO
Guy Who Knows

Anonymous